Chapter One

Becky gazed at her reflection in the mirror and smiled delightedly. She'd never worn anything like this dress before – it was beautiful. She bounced on her toes slightly, and watched the layers of silky skirts ruffle and flounce. It was fab!

"Ftand ftill a minute, dear," muttered the dressmaker through a mouthful of pins. "Jutht need to get the hem level." She crawled round Becky on her knees, adding a pin here and there.

It was the final fitting for the dresses that the triplets were to wear as bridesmaids at their Auntie Jan's wedding in three weeks' time. Becky was really excited – none of the triplets had been bridesmaids before, and she and Annabel had been talking about it for ages.

Carefully making sure she didn't move a muscle from the neck down, Becky glanced over at Annabel – her dress had been adjusted first, and now she was peacocking in front of the mirrors that surrounded the workroom, clearly even more entranced than Becky was. Annabel had played Cinderella in the school pantomime last term, and had a beautiful costume, but this dress was even better.

Auntie Jan was a journalist for a smart homes magazine, and she was *very* stylish. Her wedding was being perfectly designed down to the very last rose petal, and everything was colour-coordinated. Auntie Jan's dress was going to be made of silver-grey raw silk and she was going to have flowers in shades of purple and mauve, and an amethyst tiara. So the triplets' dresses had silvery-white bodices with lilac-coloured skirts to match.

Triplets

Becky's Dress Disaster

HOLLY WEBB

SCHOLASTIC

Scholastic Children's Books
An imprint of Scholastic Ltd
Euston House, 24 Eversholt Street
London, NW1 1DB, UK
Registered office: Westfield Road, Southam, Warwickshire, CV47 0RA
SCHOLASTIC and associated logos are trademarks and/or registered trademarks of
Scholastic Inc.

First published in the UK by Scholastic Ltd, 2005
This edition published by Scholastic Ltd, 2014

ISBN 978 1407 14480 1

British Library Cataloguing-in-Publication Data.
A CIP catalogue record for this book is available from the British Library.

This is a work of fiction. Names, characters, places, incidents and dialogues are products
of the author's imagination or are used fictitiously. Any resemblance to actual people,
living or dead, events or locales is entirely coincidental.

www.scholastic.co.uk

Becky looked at her reflection again, almost shyly – it seemed hard to believe that the princess-like figure in the mirror was her! The silvery-white fabric of the dress brought out the deep blue of her eyes, and made her long golden-blonde hair all sparkly. Next to her Annabel seemed to be thinking the same thing. As the dressmaker heaved herself up off her knees with a sigh, Annabel tiptoed over, moving super-carefully in the precious dress. She stood close to Becky and they gazed at the effect of the gorgeous, identical dresses.

"We look fantastic," said Annabel smugly. She'd never had a problem with false modesty.

Becky grinned at her – she'd never have said it herself, but yes, they did! She looked over her shoulder for Katie, wanting her to share in the excitement. Her other triplet was standing in the corner, waiting for the dressmaker to make the alterations to her dress, and she looked about as unexcited as Becky had ever seen her. In fact, she looked downright sulky. She'd kept her trainers on, and she was irritably scraping the toe of one back and forth on the carpet, and not even looking at herself in the mirror!

"Katie!" Annabel hissed. "Come over here! I want to see all of us together!"

Katie looked round, and shrugged, and just then the dressmaker, who'd been consulting with Mum about something, bustled back over with her pins and shooed Katie towards the centre of the room.

"This is really so exciting," she continued, still talking to Mum. "I've made dresses for twins before, but never triplets, and they're so completely identical! No one will be able to tell them apart in these frocks."

Mum smiled, but cast a slightly worried glance over at the triplets. They generally weren't keen on dressing alike — she'd had tantrums from them before about wearing matching outfits that their Gran had sent them.

Katie stomped grimly into the middle and stood there, looking as unlike a bridesmaid as it was possible to do in a sticky-out net-skirted dress. She looked like she was going to bite the next person who mentioned the word wedding.

Becky sighed. Katie just wasn't a dress person – and as for crystal jewellery, and posies, and high-heeled lilac satin slippers. . . She moaned every time they had to go to a dress fitting, and whenever Auntie Jan rang up with more wedding ideas she rolled her eyes horribly, but Becky hadn't quite realized how much she *meant* it. Looking at her now, Becky was starting to feel a teensy bit worried. Katie wasn't going to scowl like that all the way through the wedding, was she. . .?

Annabel didn't seem to have noticed the danger signs. "Katie! You've still got your trainers on, you muppet! You need to put the proper shoes on, or the dress won't hang right!" She clicked her tongue exasperatedly, and exchanged an "honestly!" look with the dressmaker.

Katie sullenly went back to get the high-heeled shoes that the dressmaker had lent them to try on with the dresses, and Becky nudged Annabel. "Do you think she's OK?"

Annabel gave her a blank look. Most of her brain was filled with sparkly net just now.

Becky went on trying to explain, although she had a suspicion that Annabel wasn't actually capable of processing the idea that someone could not like this dress. "She looks – cross."

Annabel gave Katie a vague glance. "No, she's OK. She's just bored standing around, that's all. Look, Becky, do you think that this dress needs something – I don't know, more twinkly about it? I wish Auntie Jan had gone for that bead decoration I pointed out to her in last month's *Brides* magazine. It would have just added that extra *something*." Annabel pirouetted in front of the mirror, scowling thoughtfully. Perhaps she could . . . no, that wouldn't be fair . . . but then again . . . the other two wouldn't mind, would they? Deep in her daydreams of crystal beads, she entirely failed to register Katie's miserable face, and the concern in Becky's eyes.

Mum didn't seem to have spotted Katie's bad mood either – she was inspecting the prices of shoes and tiaras and things, and looking slightly worried.

It was definitely up to Becky to do something. She left Annabel trying to work out from which side she looked nicest, and went over to Katie, carefully gathering up the skirt of her dress – it wasn't finally sewn yet, and it was delicate. She edged around the dressmaker, who was measuring Katie's hemline, and stood next to her sister, mulling over the best way to cheer her up. Of course – Katie had been at football practice that morning, and she'd been trying to explain Mrs Ross's new team strategy to them all in the car on the way into town earlier, but Becky hadn't really understood it. Well, she hadn't exactly been concentrating – she tended to zone out when Katie went into football-speak. Now she decided to sacrifice herself. "Katie?"

"Mmm?" It was partly a growl.

"You know that football thing you were telling us about earlier? The thing Mrs Ross is doing?"

"Mmm?" Slightly less growly, but a bit suspicious-sounding.

"Well, can you tell me about it again, 'cause I didn't get it."

Katie brightened up, and automatically unslumped herself.

"That'th lovely, dear, jutht like that," murmured the dressmaker, who'd been trying to get her to stand up straight for ages.

Katie twitched irritably, but ignored the impulse to kick the stupid dress out of her way. Eagerly she beckoned her sister closer, and Becky gave a secret sigh of relief. Katie had taken the bait. Now, if she could just keep her amused for the rest of the fitting, Katie might forget how bored she was with the whole process. Becky screwed up her face in concentration and prepared to get her head round the complicated explanation that Katie was clearly about to launch into.

"OK, so which bit didn't you understand?" Katie asked enthusiastically.

"All of it," said Becky firmly. She might as well do it properly – in for a penny, in for a pound, as Mum sometimes said.

"Well, Mrs Ross reckons we need to learn to be more versatile. She reckons that if we understand how every player in the team works, then we'll know what to expect from them, right?"

"Ye-es," agreed Becky cautiously. This sounded like sense as far as she could see – Katie hadn't gone into football gobbledegook yet.

"OK, so obviously a striker plays really

differently to a defender, yes? And a goalie is just like another kind of thing altogether, so it's really difficult adjusting to the different style of play, but it's going to be completely excellent because. . ." Becky drifted slightly here. She'd caught sight of herself in The Dress (it definitely had capital letters) in the mirror, and she was imagining what her boyfriend, David, would think if he could see her. She smiled happily to herself. There were bound to be loads of photos taken at the wedding. Maybe she could give one of them to David? She had a picture of him that had been taken by chance at the triplets' birthday party last term, but she didn't think he had a photo of her except for silly ones on his phone. She imagined him putting it in a frame and keeping it in his room, and it gave her a little glow inside. Then she jumped – Katie had stopped and was giving her an enquiring look. Becky shot a panicky glance from side to side, but there was no one to help her out, so she plumped for a fifty–fifty chance.

"Oh yes! Definitely!" she exclaimed, nodding furiously, and gazing hopefully at Katie.

Katie looked a bit surprised. She'd just asked Becky if she wanted to meet up with her and Megan in the park the next day so she could demonstrate what she'd been talking about, and she *really* hadn't expected such an enthusiastic reaction.

"Cool! I said to Megan that we'd meet up tomorrow afternoon – she's going to show me some of her goalie moves and I'm giving her pointers on passing. You can try and put some shots past me too!"

Becky realized too late what she'd got herself into and thought fast. "Is it OK if Fran comes too? I said I'd go for a long walk with her and Feathers tomorrow." Actually this had only been a vague suggestion rather than a plan, but Becky reckoned having Fran and Feathers around for the football training session might make it a lot more fun.

"Course!" Katie sounded so happy that Becky felt a little bit guilty. But at least she'd got her sister out of the glooms, that was the important thing.

And with perfect timing, the dressmaker slid the last pin into the hem of Katie's dress. "Done. You look lovely, dear."

Katie just sniffed, and raced – as much as she could in a floor-length dress – to get changed.

Mum spotted her and realized that the fitting was finished. "Oh good – can you two go and get changed as well? Then we can have a look at all the other bits you need."

Annabel had looked mutinous at the idea of taking the gorgeous creation off, but when Mrs Ryan mentioned accessories she moved nearly as fast as Katie had, and it wasn't long before all three triplets were back in their own clothes and gathering round their mother.

Becky grinned to herself as she saw Katie.

Now that her sister was wearing her own jeans, trainers and purple hooded fleecy top, she looked like she could breathe again. Of course the dress hadn't actually been made with a corset, but it just seemed to have that effect on Katie. It *was* nice to be able to move without panicking that you were going to tread on the dress, or tear it, or do something else awful, though. Becky felt a bit more relaxed now that she was back in her own green cords and favourite cat T-shirt. Annabel was the only one of the three of them who looked as though she'd felt more comfortable in the dress than she did in her own denim skirt, stripy tights and silver Kickers, Becky mused. Although Bel loved those boots so much that Becky was surprised she wasn't arguing to wear them to the wedding – after all, they'd fit in with Auntie Jan's silver and lilac theme. . .

But now, Bel was looking blissed out by the selection of shoes that was currently being waved under her nose. Mum usually wasn't that keen on the triplets wearing high-heeled shoes, but the wedding seemed to have put that out of her mind. Apparently, heels were a necessity for bridesmaids, although Katie did try and argue for the pretty and, more importantly, *flat* ballet pumps. Annabel was disgusted.

"Katie! Those are for *three year olds*! Are you mad?"

"No!" Katie snapped back. "I just don't fancy breaking my neck in *those*!" She glared crossly at the strappy, silver, high-heeled sandals that Annabel was ogling. "And have you forgotten that this wedding is in the middle of April? Those are going to be really fun if it pours with rain."

"It won't," said Annabel with supreme confidence.

"How do you know?" Katie asked, slightly disconcerted by Annabel's certainty.

"*Because*. It just won't."

Katie smirked, and Mum decided it was definitely time to intervene. "I do think those are a bit too summery, Bel. But these ones are nice, don't you think?" She held up a pair they'd seen already, that actually looked a bit like the ballet shoes, only with small heels. "They're very like the ones you wanted, Katie," Mum continued, in a peacemaking tone of voice. "Becky? What do you think? Do you like them?"

"Yes, they're sweet." Becky was uncomfortably aware that she might just have got on the wrong side of both sisters at once – the shoes were pretty, but they weren't nearly glamorous enough for Bel, and they were far too fancy for Katie. As Mum and the dressmaker decided that those were definitely the right ones, Becky sighed. Annabel and Katie were still muttering insults at each other. ("You're crazy!" "Well, you look like you bought all your clothes at a jumble sale – a really bad jumble sale!") She had a feeling that this wasn't going to be the only time between now and the wedding that she would be playing piggy in the middle. . .

Chapter Two

Katie and Annabel were still glaring at each other by the time they got in the car, and when they reached home Katie stomped up the garden path looking like a stormcloud. Becky felt decidedly irritated. All her good work listening to football stuff wasted! *And* she had to go and be coached by Katie and Megan tomorrow!

As Mum unlocked the door they heard the phone start to ring. Katie dashed in to answer it, and then walked out into the hall with her hand over it. "It's for you, Mum." She sounded puzzled. "It's a man – someone I don't know."

"Oh!" Mrs Ryan went pink, and gestured

urgently for Katie to give her the phone. Then she shooed the girls out of her way and went into the living room, shutting the door behind her.

Annabel and Katie's spat was immediately forgotten – something important was clearly going on here, much more important than disagreements over shoes. The three of them exchanged a look, and crept over to listen at the door. OK, so it wasn't any of their business who Mum was talking to, but they had a horrible suspicion and they wanted to know for sure! Unfortunately, they couldn't really hear much, even with their ears squashed painfully against the door. They could tell that Mum sounded excited, though, and luckily they could just about make out when she was saying goodbye, as that gave them the chance to beetle into the kitchen and stand around looking casual.

It was lucky that Mrs Ryan was still preoccupied with her phone call, otherwise the triplets' consciously disinterested poses would have struck her as very suspicious. As it was, she ignored the fact that Becky was studiously reading the financial section of the newspaper, and that Katie and Annabel were apparently fascinated by the milk in the door of the fridge.

"Girls, I hope it's OK, but I'm planning to go out this evening, with . . . a friend. We're going to have dinner, and I've arranged for Mrs Lucy from next door to come and look after you while I'm out." Mrs Ryan had almost said babysit, but then remembered just in time that Annabel tended to go ballistic when anyone implied she still needed babysitting. She looked thoughtfully at her daughters. How much should she tell them? Maybe it was time to let them know what was going on – they were far too old to have secrets kept from them. She smiled to herself. Annabel had looked like a teenager, posing with that beautiful dress on earlier in the afternoon.

She looked round at them all – and got three intrigued stares back. Oh, they knew something was going on all right! She smiled, and took a deep breath. "Actually, this friend is the dad of someone you know." She failed to pick up Katie's horrified glance at the other two, and Annabel's indrawn breath – they'd been right! "Jeff Cooper – Max's dad." Mrs Ryan met Katie's gaze this time, and flinched slightly. "Oh, yes. I'd forgotten you had that little run-in with him, Katie."

The triplets looked disbelievingly at her. How could she have forgotten? Max had nearly broken Katie's leg!

Mrs Ryan looked at them a little worriedly. "I won't be out late. You like Mrs Lucy, don't you?"

They nodded slowly. It wasn't Mrs Lucy who was the problem! They'd suspected for a while that Mum had been getting on far too well with Max's dad, and they had even been pretty sure that he'd sent her a Valentine's card, but they'd had no idea it had got this far. Once Katie had told the others what she thought was going on — she and Megan had been the first to spot it — telling the story had taken such a weight off her mind that she'd almost managed to convince herself that the whole thing had fizzled out. It was over a month since Valentine's Day and nothing had happened, after all.

Mum started getting stuff ready for their tea, so the triplets disappeared quickly in case she decided to ask for help. They didn't mind helping usually, but they needed to talk this over. They sped up to their room and huddled on Annabel's bed.

"This is a disaster!' proclaimed Annabel dramatically.

Normally Katie would have told her off for being a drama queen, but she felt pretty much the same way at the moment. She nodded dolefully. "How *can* she go out with him? Imagine, it's like one of us going out with Max!"

Annabel groaned realistic sick noises, but Becky shrugged. "Maybe he's not like Max – I mean, Mum wouldn't go out with him if he wasn't nice."

The other two looked at her disbelievingly, and shook their heads. Annabel folded her arms. "All I can say is, Mum's gone mad – and maybe you have too, Becky! Max's dad! Nice!" She and Katie rolled their eyes at each other.

Becky glared. "I'm not saying it's not a disaster – you know I can't stand Max – you just never know, that's all."

That was true, at least. The triplets sighed, and slumped back on to the bed, pondering the general unfairness of life. . .

The triplets were rather silent that evening. Mrs Lucy, who enjoyed babysitting for them, as they were normally very happy to sit down and play silly games like Pictionary, or try to teach her how to use the PlayStation, found them a bit of a puzzle. She eventually persuaded them into a game of Trivial Pursuit, but when she found that Katie was actually getting the sport questions all wrong, she realized that they just weren't concentrating.

"Are you three all right?" she asked, putting the cards back into the box. "You don't seem to be having much fun tonight."

Becky gave her an apologetic smile. "We're OK – Mum's gone out with someone we don't like very much, that's all."

"Huh!" Katie didn't so much say this as spit it. "*That's* a nice way of putting it."

"We've never actually met him, you know," Becky pointed out reasonably. It was a bad idea – Katie wasn't up for reasonableness right now.

"Don't need to meet him," she snapped. "If he's Max's dad he's got to be horrible, it's just common sense, which you obviously haven't got any of."

Mrs Lucy looked shocked. "Katie!"

Katie shrugged, and muttered, "Sorry," without even looking at her sister.

Becky tried hard not to mind – it was understandable that Katie would be extra-furious about Mr Cooper, after all her scraps with Max – but did she really need to be so hurtful about it? Becky had only been trying to calm things down. She stared down at her hands and very carefully put all the little wedges back into their bag, trying not to let the tears get any further than the corners of her eyes. It was bad enough having to deal with Mum having a horrible new boyfriend, without it meaning a cross, snappish sister as well.

Annabel gave Katie a look of surprise – normally she was very protective of Becky, and if Annabel had made a comment like that Katie would probably have given her a real telling-off. She decided not to say anything though – she didn't feel like a fight, and Katie seemed to be itching for one right now.

*

That night, for once, the triplets didn't chat for ages when they went to bed. Usually they ended up gradually falling asleep mid-gossip at the weekends (during the week Mum came in and shut them up). But no one was quite in the mood tonight. Becky lay awake listening for the telltale click of the door-latch, and Mum and Mrs Lucy's whispered conversation, followed by Mum coming up to bed really, really quietly. It was something Becky'd always done, ever since she could first remember her parents going out and leaving them with someone. After all, what if something happened to them while they were out? Becky knew it was stupid really, but it was a hard habit to break. And tonight it sounded like Katie was doing it too, because as soon as the door went Becky heard her sister sigh and turn over.

Mum didn't mention anything about her date when the triplets finally surfaced quite late the next morning, but Becky thought she looked particularly happy. It was really sad, Becky thought, that something that was obviously making their mum feel good should make them so miserable. Katie came down to breakfast in a tracksuit and trainers, and seemed surprised that Becky was wearing a skirt.

"You can't practise in that!"

Becky tried to protest. "We're not going to the park till this afternoon!"

But Katie looked so pleading that she trailed back upstairs to put a pair of tracksuit bottoms on. Becky had a feeling it was going to be a long day. She hadn't had much time for homework the day before because of the dress-fitting, so she spent the morning slogging through her maths and science, which Katie, of course, had whizzed through on Friday night, as they were her best subjects. She hadn't seen Annabel do any homework at all, but then Bel always seemed to get by on a snatched five minutes here and there.

She fitted in a quick call to Fran to break the news that they would be joining football training. She'd been prepared to grovel, but Fran didn't mind. She was an only child and she lived just with her dad, so she loved doing stuff with the triplets – there was always so much going on in their house.

"And I've got the worst news as well," Becky added, after she'd explained the football stuff.

"What?" Fran was intrigued.

"You remember that thing we thought was going on with Mum and Max's dad?"

"Uh-huh."

"They went out on a date last night!"

Fran let out a suitably horrified gasp. "No!"

'Yup. So watch out for Katie – she's in and out of the world's worst mood. Hopefully some football will cheer her up."

Megan's dad dropped her at the triplets' house just after lunch – they'd arranged to meet Fran and Feathers at the park, as her house was just on the other side of it. Katie and Megan were looking sickeningly energetic, Becky thought, yawning after her late night lying awake. They dashed round the house finding footballs, and boots, and a million and one other things that Becky really couldn't see the point of. *And* it seemed to be her job to carry half of them. Annabel stood watching, nibbling blissfully on a piece of peanut butter toast, and smirking at Becky.

"Why don't you come too, Bel?" asked Megan, enthusiasm practically bubbling out of her ears.

"Sorry, Megan, I'm really busy this afternoon," Annabel replied earnestly. Then she grinned, and fluttered her fingers at them. "Got some heavy-duty manicuring to do."

Katie and Megan shook their heads in disbelief and Becky glared at Annabel. "I hope you've done your maths homework," she said crossly. "You needn't think you're going to 'borrow' mine like you did last week."

Katie looked shocked. "You let her copy your homework?"

"No! Well, I suppose so. She said she just wanted to check she was on the right lines."

"Mmm, and if I'd borrowed yours, Katie, Mr Jones would have noticed for sure." Annabel nodded seriously. "You get them all right. Becky and me normally get the same kind of stuff totally wrong."

Katie and Becky exchanged long-suffering glances, and left her to it.

Deepdene Park was only five minutes' walk from the triplets' house, and they'd been going there since they were tiny. It had a gorgeous little pond with loads of ducks and a couple of swans, and plenty of open space for football practice, even if it didn't have a proper pitch. It was also a paradise for dogs, as there were quite a few little woody bits, and some long grass. When Becky, Katie and Megan arrived, Becky took a quick look round. No Fran, as far as she could see – but then a golden shape launched itself out of the trees a little way away and came bounding towards her at what looked like the speed of light, barking its head off.

"Watch out! Dog incoming!" yelled the black-haired person racing after him, and the three girls dropped all their stuff and prepared to field Feathers.

He was obviously in a very good mood – well, he always was, except on visits to the V–E–T – and he wanted to share it with them all, especially Becky, whom he adored. He waltzed round them, his whole body wagging along with his tail, and tried to lick as much person as he possibly could. Fran panted up after him, and tried to grab his collar, and eventually she and Becky got him calmed down enough to put his lead back on.

"Sorry!" Fran gasped. "He didn't get much of a walk yesterday 'cause me and Dad were out, so he's gone hyper today. Did he break anything?"

Much as Fran adored Feathers, she lived in

constant fear of him doing something awful. He was a lovely dog, very sweet-natured, but very big, very stupid, and very excitable. He lived for food and chasing things, and he tended to ignore whatever got in his way, like people . . . or furniture. He had a special talent for finding whichever table had china on it, and walking through it, hard.

Katie looked down at the furry whirlwind who was now chasing his own tail. "I thought Golden Retrievers were supposed to be really obedient."

"Mmmm," Becky and Fran agreed with her.

"And sensible."

"Uh-huh."

"Guide dogs are Golden Retrievers lots of the time."

"Yup."

"So?"

Fran grinned. "Feathers thinks he's a Chihuahua. That's why he bumps into things all the time."

Katie frowned. "Is he going to behave while we practise?"

"Can't he join in?" asked Becky hopefully. "He's good at football. Don't you remember when Fran brought him round?"

Katie sighed, and shrugged. "Oh, I suppose so. But if he runs off with the ball, I'm not chasing after him, OK? You two can do it."

"Absolutely." Becky nodded vigorously. "He'll be really good, Katie, honestly. He's a great striker – we'll use him to test you out!" She and Fran giggled.

Actually, Feathers *was* really good at football – the problem was he didn't like letting go of the ball, and passing, obviously, was something he didn't get. Why on earth would he want to give this lovely ball to *someone else*? But chasing him round the field was certainly good exercise, and after fifteen minutes of Feathersball, the girls slumped down on the grass for a rest.

"Well, he's definitely winning," sighed

Katie, leaning back on her elbows, and watching Feathers, who'd let go of the ball for once so he could stand a few centimetres away and bark frantically at it, in case it was thinking of running away.

Fran looked apologetic. "Sorry! Me and Becky'll take him for a run when we've caught our breath, and then you and Megan can practise properly."

Becky gave her a quick, relieved glance. Thank goodness! Katie and Megan were so serious about their football that practising with them could be a bit scary.

Five minutes later, Katie heaved herself up off the ground, and gave Megan a hand to pull her up. "We'll see you two in a bit then."

"Uh-huh. Maybe once we've worn Feathers out a bit we can come back and you can show us some more of the stuff," said Becky, trying to sound enthusiastic. She felt a teensy bit guilty when Katie looked so pleased.

Becky, Fran and Feathers headed off to the woodier part of the park so Feathers could go squirrel-chasing – his second-favourite game after football. Becky and Fran chatted as Feathers raced ahead of them, woofing ecstatically.

"Oh, look at that gorgeous dog!" Becky exclaimed suddenly, pointing a little way ahead. It was a small Jack Russell terrier, racing through the long grass after a Frisbee that his owner had just thrown for him. The dog was pretty tiny, and the grass was long, so he wasn't so much running as bouncing, covering the distance in great bounds as he fought to get his nose out of the grass and see where the Frisbee was going.

The girls laughed delightedly as the little dog leaped into the air at just the right moment to catch the Frisbee – which wasn't much smaller than he was – and turned in mid-air to race back to his owner for another go. On the way back they couldn't even see the dog –

there was just a bright-yellow Frisbee bouncing up and down above the grass.

"Ohhh, he's so cute," said Fran. "I wish Feathers would fetch."

"He does!" said Becky, surprised.

"Yeah, but the point of fetching is that the dog gives it back. Feather fetches and then disappears off to chew the stick into a million pieces. That one's obviously going to give the Frisbee to his owner." Fran and Becky's eyes tracked the tiny dog back, and then they both gasped.

"Oh!" Becky looked as though she couldn't believe what she was seeing. "That – that isn't *Max*, is it?"

"Yup." Fran nodded, equally gobsmacked.

The Jack Russell had handed over the Frisbee, after a little bit of mock-growling, and was now being made a huge fuss of by a dark-haired boy who Becky and Fran never normally saw without a scowl on his face. Max Cooper – the triplets' least favourite person.

(He was definitely beating Amy Mannering at the moment, since this whole thing between the triplets' mum and his dad.)

Fran and Becky moved slightly so that they were behind some bushes and could watch without Max seeing them.

"Max is being really nice," murmured Becky, disbelievingly.

She could see that he adored the little dog from the way he was patting him, and the dog was jumping all over him, licking and yapping as though he was having the best time ever. It was weird. This was *Max*. But Becky just didn't feel like she could hate somebody who was so obviously such a caring dog-owner. She met Fran's confused green eyes, and they stared at each other in amazement. Max couldn't be nice – it just didn't make sense!

Chapter Three

On Monday morning, Becky sat at the breakfast table paying hardly any attention to her toast, or the conversation that Mum, Katie and Annabel were deep in, about what Mum ought to get from the supermarket that morning. She was still turning over Max's strange behaviour in her mind. Really, she supposed it *wasn't* strange behaviour – it was perfectly normal to be nice to your dog. But since when did Max ever behave like a normal human being? *That* was what was so weird.

"Becky? Becky!"

She jumped as Katie prodded her. "What?"

"For the third time, do we need any cat food?" Katie was looking at her as though she was totally dim. "What's the matter, anyway?"

Becky hadn't told Katie or Annabel about the odd encounter with Max — Katie disliked him so much that it would probably have just brought back her bad mood, and Becky really wanted to avoid that. She hated it when people argued, and Katie had such a strong character that her moods tended to affect the whole house. "Nothing," she said hurriedly. "I was just thinking." She caught sight of Pixie, their little black ex-stray, who was slinking round the legs of Katie's chair in the hope of a bit of dropped toast. She didn't actually like toast, but she loved butter, and her rough little tongue was very efficient at licking it off. "I was trying to remember when we last put flea-stuff on the cats. And, no, we've got lots of cat food."

Pixie gave her such an accusing look that Becky could have sworn the skinny black cat had understood what she'd said. Pixie never thought they had enough food. It was to do with being a stray once, Becky thought. Pixie was never quite convinced that the next meal wasn't going to be her last. The Ryans' other cat, Orlando, a big ginger tom, didn't have that excuse. He was just plain greedy, and he had a big furry marmalade tummy to show for it.

Before Katie had interrupted her, Becky had been gradually coming to the conclusion that maybe she ought to say something to Max. After all, however much Katie might hate the idea, their mum *was* going out with his dad – they were going to have to talk to each other sometime. At least the episode with the dog had made that seem less of a problem, because now Becky felt she actually had something in common with Max – it made him seem a bit less scary, somehow.

Not that much less, though. As Becky walked into their classroom when the bell went, she was practically shaking.

"What's the matter?" asked Fran curiously. "You look all trembly. Are you ill?" she added in a worried voice.

"No," Becky muttered. "I'm just trying to make myself say hello to Max. Ask him about his dog maybe. With all that stuff I told you about my mum and his dad, it's just stupid not to talk to each other."

Fran nodded, but slowly, and she didn't look quite convinced. She wasn't really sure this was a good idea – not for shy Becky anyway. Still, she certainly wasn't going to stop her. What she *was* going to do was make sure she was there too, in case Max didn't share Becky's good intentions. . . She followed the determined little figure of her friend over to the other side of the room, where Max was sitting on his own reading a football magazine. He seemed to have had a bust-up with his mate Ben – certainly they didn't sit together much any more.

"Hi Max," said Becky, but so nervously it came out in a whisper.

Max looked up, and immediately scowled at her. "What do *you* want?" he snapped.

Becky tried to stay calm. After all, she

reasoned to herself, if Max had unexpectedly come to say something nice to her, she would probably have reacted in just the same way. She smiled at him, and ploughed on. "Me and Fran saw you in the park yesterday. With your dog – he's really cute! Have you had him long? I didn't know you had a dog." She stammered to a halt. Max's angry, white face was not exactly giving her the impression that he wanted to swap pet-care tips.

Max shoved his chair back with a snarl that made everyone else in the class look round in surprise, and Fran move in shoulder to shoulder with Becky.

"What's it to you?" he growled furiously at Becky. "Why are you so interested all of a sudden? You needn't think I'm going to be all friendly with you just because your stupid mother's trying to cosy up to my dad." He was looming over her angrily, and Becky cowered. She hadn't really expected him to be all sweetness and light, but she certainly hadn't been ready for this ferocious attack. It looked like Max and Katie felt pretty much the same about the whole parents dating thing. . .

Suddenly, there *was* Katie, as furious as Max, and backed up by Annabel, her pretty face frowning.

"What's going on?" Katie demanded sharply. "Don't you dare shout at my sister like that, she hasn't done anything to you."

"She's over here, isn't she? Bugging me! Why don't you all just get lost, you lot *and* your mum!" Max was practically nose-to-nose with Katie now.

Watching in horror, Becky thought she could almost see Katie's hackles rise at the mention of their mother. She seemed to get taller, and her deep-blue eyes took on a steely glint.

"Since when was this part of the classroom your property? My sister can walk anywhere she likes, and so can I. Like this." And Katie shoved forward, forcing Max to retreat or be pushed over. Max stepped back, surprised. "And if there happens to be something in my way," she continued sweetly, "then I'm just going to walk on it. Like *this*." She trampled decidedly on Max's jumper, which had been lying next to his rucksack, and smiled at him, nastily.

Annabel and Fran were looking pretty horrified now as well, as were Megan and Saima who'd come to see what was going on. What on earth had got into Katie? She was behaving like – well, like Max!

The whole class was watching in a breathless hush, waiting to see what Max would do, when a cold voice snapped. "Go to your seats, all of you. Max, pick up your jumper and sit down." Miss Fraser had arrived – just in time, Becky thought. "Not you, Katie," their class teacher added, her usually friendly voice still sounding icy. "Go and stand by my desk, I'll talk to you later."

Registration was torture for Becky. She

could only imagine how embarrassed and upset Katie must be feeling, standing at the front of the classroom with everyone staring at her. Although, actually, Katie didn't look embarrassed at all. She looked like the heroine in a film, about to be executed by firing squad for standing up for what she believed in. Becky shuddered. Katie was in trouble for standing up for *her*. *But I didn't ask her to!* a tiny voice inside her muttered indignantly. *She didn't have to come storming in like that, like she always does*. She sighed. She'd never have thought a few months ago that she'd get sick of having Katie look after her.

She looked carefully round the class, to see what people's faces were saying. Annabel was picking at her rubber anxiously, looking at Katie. Becky caught her eye and they exchanged worried shrugs. *What was all that about?*

Becky moved on. Huh. Of course. Amy Mannering and her mates Emily and Cara were smirking and whispering behind their hands to each other. Cara saw her watching and sneered, and Becky looked away quickly, and by chance caught sight of Max. She'd been avoiding looking at him — why on earth had he got so mad with her? She'd only been trying to be nice, after all. She sighed to herself. Somehow, her peace-loving idea of all of them being friendly seemed pretty stupid. Now that she'd accidentally glanced at Max, though, she found herself drawn back to look again, feeling confused. Max ought to be sitting there looking insufferable, grinning all over his face. He'd just had an argument with Katie Ryan, his worst enemy, and *she* was in big trouble while he'd got off scot free! So why was he looking so miserable? His shoulders were all hunched up, and he was staring down at his homework diary as though his life depended on it.

Becky chewed the end of her biro thoughtfully. Max reminded her of someone, but she just couldn't work out who. Something about that determined refusal to look at anybody, so no one could be horrible. . .

She suddenly sat bolt upright, and got a confused glare from Annabel. Of course! Max looked like her! At the beginning of last term when she'd been rowing with Katie and Annabel, and not really known anybody at their new school, she'd sat in all her classes just like that, hoping everyone would forget she was there. Was that what was happening to Max now? Poor Max — it was such an awful feeling. She still remembered what it was like, even though she had loads of mates now: Fran; her sisters, of course, and their best mates Megan and Saima; even Jack and Robin were fun. And David — she grinned at him across the table, thinking how lucky she was. He gave her a strange, serious look in return. Becky felt confused for a moment, but then realized that he must be surprised to see her looking so happy when Katie was in trouble. She wished she could explain, but she certainly wasn't going to risk whispering when Miss Fraser was already cross.

Miss Fraser kept Katie behind when the bell went for first lesson, so Annabel and Becky waited outside for her and sent the others off to save seats. Becky was expecting David to wait too, and she was intending to explain why she'd smiled at him, but he disappeared off, leaving her feeling confused. Where was he going? They normally sat with each other in maths. She was still gazing up the corridor after him, looking troubled, when Katie stalked out of their classroom with a defiant expression on her face.

"So what happened?" asked Annabel interestedly as they set off to maths. "It sounded like she was having a massive go at you."

"Mmm," Katie agreed. "She put me in detention for tomorrow. She said I was bullying him! Can you imagine? Max!" She sounded indignant.

Becky frowned. Max had bullied her practically since she'd started at Manor Hill, and Katie and the others had always stood up for her. But it had never been quite like this. Just when did always hating and fighting with somebody you thought was really mean turn into bullying *them*? Maybe when they stopped fighting back, and looked as miserable and alone as Max had just now. . . She looked at Katie, still raging to Bel about how unfair it was that Max hadn't got detention too. Katie was always scrupulously fair, but it seemed to Becky that she was so upset about the situation with Mum that she couldn't see what was really going on. Max might still be horrible, but he wasn't *happy*. Whenever he'd quarrelled with Katie before – or been picking on Becky – he'd been enjoying himself, and Becky had actually been frightened of him. As she'd watched Katie kicking his jumper along the floor earlier, she'd just felt sorry for him as she recognized the trapped, bewildered look on his face.

Annabel didn't seem to have noticed any of this, although she did say, "What were you doing kicking his sweater all over the floor like that? You'd have gone mad at anyone who did something like that to one of us."

Katie shrugged crossly. "Oh, he deserved it, Bel. Come on, he did, didn't he?"

Annabel nodded. "Mmm. Maybe. I can't believe Miss Fraser just let him off. That really isn't fair." And the two of them went on discussing how unfair it was, while Becky just listened, looking anxiously at Katie's hard face.

By the time she got to maths, Becky had turned everything over in her head so many times that her brain was feeling dizzy, and she failed to notice that David had gone to sit with Jack and Robin instead of with them. Katie, bullying Max? She just couldn't get her head round it. And as for getting Katie's head round it – huh. You might as well try getting her into a full-length meringue dress with high heels and a tiara. Oh dear. . .

It was halfway through the lesson that Becky suddenly came to (without the slightest clue about what the square of the hypotenuse was, let alone what you did with it) and noticed where David was. Or, more precisely, where he *wasn't*. Why had he gone to sit with Jack and Robin? She tried to telegraph this to him with her eyebrows, but he wasn't looking at her, and Mr Jones was, so she decided she'd better pay some attention to triangles for a bit. As soon as the bell went though, she stuffed all her books into her bag, said, "Wait for me!" to Fran and hurried over to David. She didn't realize, but it showed just how much she'd changed in the last few months. The old Becky would have panicked and agonized about what was going on for most of the day before daring to go and confront somebody.

David was pretending to be very interested in putting all his stuff away as she came up, so she plucked at his arm.

"Hey! Why didn't you come and sit with us?" She tried hard not to sound like she was upset – she just wanted to know what was going on.

He mumbled something unintelligible, still staring into the depths of his rucksack, and Becky tugged him round to face her.

"Look, what's wrong? What have I done to make you off with me like this?"

He looked up, frowning. "Isn't it obvious?"

"No!"

He looked shamefaced, as though he was realizing he'd been a bit stupid. "You were talking to Max – being all nice to him," he muttered.

"Are you jealous?" Becky almost squeaked, disbelievingly.

"No! Well . . . maybe a bit. What were you talking to him for? You hate him! I didn't know what was going on."

Becky hooked her arm through his. "Look, come on, we're going to be late for French. I'll explain on the way. Fran'll tell you, she was there," she added cryptically, as they caught up with Fran, who'd been pointing at her watch in a "come on!" kind of way. "I was just explaining to David about Max."

By the time they got to French she and Fran had filled David in. He already knew about the nightmare with Max's dad and the triplets' mum. He couldn't stand Max either. He had the same situation with him on the football team that Katie had with Cara. He just had to try and forget how much he disliked him.

"Well, I suppose trying to talk to him's a good idea," he murmured doubtfully, as they sat down in the classroom. Becky had made absolutely sure he was sitting next to her for this lesson. "I don't fancy your chances, though. I mean what did you think, he was suddenly going to decide everything was OK and you were all best mates?"

"Course not! I just reckon we ought to be able to talk to each other without starting

World War III, that's all." Becky sighed. That wasn't looking very hopeful now. Katie was still acting martyred and sulky – all Becky'd done was make her hate Max even more! "All right, I suppose it was dumb not to expect him to have a go at me."

She looked quickly over at Max, who was sharing a table with Amy, Cara and Emily. Amy looked as though she was actually being nice to him. Great – that was just what they needed. Max and Amy had been known to gang up on the triplets before, and Amy was a champion stirrer. If anyone could make him hate Katie and the others more, it was her. Altogether, so far Becky's peacemaking plan looked to have been a complete and utter disaster. . .

Chapter Four

Mum was really, really upset with Katie when the triplets got home that night and she found out about the detention. She didn't say much, but it was obvious that she was very disappointed.

Becky nibbled miserably at her thumbnail as Katie tried to defend herself.

"I wasn't bullying him, Mum! Miss Fraser got the wrong idea. He'd been picking on Becky and I stopped him, that's all. You know what he's like!"

Annabel tried to join in here to help out, but Mum just snapped at her to be quiet and went back to Katie.

"It says here that you were bullying, Katie.

Miss Fraser's not stupid, I don't see how she could get it that wrong. I really never thought I'd get a note like this about you."

The triplets slunk upstairs. Mum hadn't been telling the other two off, but they did feel responsible, Becky especially, as she'd started the whole thing.

Katie threw herself down on her bed angrily. "It's so unfair! Why am I the one getting into so much trouble? Do you think you could manage to stay away from that idiot for a while, Becky? Or at least back me up with Mum next time I'm getting told off for helping you out!"

Becky said nothing for a moment. She couldn't remember feeling so at odds with Katie for a long time, and she wasn't looking forward to her sister's reaction to what she was about to say. She didn't think Annabel was going to be particularly impressed either, actually.

"Look, I'm really sorry you got into trouble." Becky went over to the windowseat and opened the rats' cage, picking up black-and-white Cassie for a cuddle. She felt she needed the comfort of something furry to give her confidence a boost. "I just don't think you should have booted Max's jumper around the floor! You were really mean!"

"Oh great! Now you're having a go at me! Thanks a bunch, Becky, I thought at least you might have been on my side. What is it with you at the moment?"

"That's not fair!" Becky protested indignantly. "I know you were trying to help me out—" Here Katie gave a snort, but Becky ploughed on. "You were trying to help me out, and Max *was* being mean, but he didn't start it. I wanted to talk to him, 'cause I thought we should try and get on – what with everything that's been happening."

Katie's face blackened. She so didn't want to talk about this. Annabel was looking as though she couldn't believe what Becky was saying either.

Becky started to speak faster — so as to finish what she was saying before Katie stormed out, which looked like it would be fairly soon. "And I think Max is feeling very miserable—"

"Good!"

"And we ought to be nice to him!"

Katie just shook her head in disgust. "You're crazy. He's been a nightmare to you ever since we started at Manor Hill, and now you want us to be *nice* to him? Don't you remember what he did? I missed the league final because of him!"

"I know! But if Mum's going out with his dad, then—"

"Then nothing." Katie had never sounded so final. "It doesn't make any difference. I don't have to like him, and I never will."

And with that she stalked out of the room, leaving Becky gasping, and Annabel looking as though for once she didn't know what to say.

That didn't last long though. "Becky, you can't seriously want us to be friends with him? Katie's right – you must be mad!" And Annabel walked off, shaking her head disgustedly.

Becky wasn't sure what to say to Katie after the fight. When they went down for tea her sister was pretty silent, but she didn't seem to be upset with Becky, particularly. It was just as if she was having a bad day all round. As Mum was still cross about the detention, it wasn't a very cheerful meal, and Annabel and Becky felt as though they were chatting through a forcefield of gloom.

Mum had obviously made a big effort to put the problems with Katie and Max out of her mind by the next morning, and Katie seemed to be dealing with the whole situation by pretending it had never happened, so it seemed like just a normal Tuesday. Underneath though, Becky felt as though she could sense all the problems and stresses bubbling away, like some horrible poisonous stew, just waiting to boil over. It didn't help that Max spent that whole day taking every opportunity to spit insults at whichever triplet was nearest. By the end of school on Wednesday, Katie had taken to digging her nails into the palms of her hands to stop herself snapping back at him – she really didn't want to get into trouble and upset Mum again, however much she knew she was right. . .

Becky was still a bit worried about Katie and the wedding as well. She'd almost forgotten about that, with the whole Max nightmare, but then she got a nasty reminder on Thursday evening. She was sitting on the sofa watching a vet programme on TV, and vaguely listening to Mum on the phone in the background. Becky shuddered as she heard Mum enthusing to Auntie Jan about her latest date with Jeff Cooper. Things were going really well, apparently. Mum sounded really happy. Oh, why couldn't she have found someone to date who didn't come with added disgusting boy? It wasn't fair.

Mum and Auntie Jan were now discussing the exact shade of lilac tulips for her wedding bouquet, and it was just then that Katie wandered into the room, heard something about the merits of lavender ribbons versus silver, gave a disgusted snort and stomped out again. Becky gazed after her worriedly, and decided maybe it was time to try asking Annabel for help.

"Bel!"

Her sister was practically sitting in Mum's lap, trying to hear both sides of the phone conversation. "Ssshhhhh!"

"Bel, I really need to talk to you about Katie – do you think she's going to be OK when Auntie Jan comes this weekend?" Auntie Jan was coming for the day on Saturday so that they could go and pick up the bridesmaids' dresses together, and choose all the finishing touches, including the jewellery.

"What do you mean? Why shouldn't she be?"

"Well, she wasn't exactly a bundle of laughs at the last fitting was she? What if she loses it and upsets Auntie Jan?"

Annabel flapped a hand distractedly – the words *crystal drops* had just been mentioned, and she was terrified that she was missing something important. "Oh, Becky, stop fussing!"

But Becky couldn't. Now that Katie was bottling up everything with Max, she had a horrible feeling that a weekend of dresses and wedding chatter just might make her even worse. Annabel was obviously going to be useless though. She was so excited about the wedding – which was only just over two weeks away now – that it seemed pointless trying to get her to help. She certainly wasn't the right person to distract Katie from dresses, when she was spending all her time at school discussing them with Saima, and at home

61

drawing more and more complicated and expensive-looking creations of her own.

The thing was, apart from her worries about Katie, Becky was really looking forward to the weekend – she was almost as desperate as Annabel to see the finished dresses, and going to the florist with Auntie Jan to choose flowers for their posies sounded great. The smart country house where the wedding was being held was close to Stallford, so Auntie Jan was using a florist in the town.

Becky was determined not to let her niggling worry about Katie spoil all the fun. Maybe the excited weddingy atmosphere would get to her by Saturday? Becky tried to banish it from her mind, and by Friday she was nearly as excited as Annabel, spending most of their Geography lesson peering over her shoulder with Saima and Fran, looking at her sister's elegant jewellery designs. It was unlikely that the wedding budget would run to that number of diamonds, but it was fun to dream!

"Can I borrow that a minute?" Fran hissed, flicking a quick glance at Mrs Travers, their super-dull Geography teacher, who was drawing very complicated and boring diagrams of rock-formations on the whiteboard. Amazingly enough, Katie actually seemed to find them more interesting than the diamonds.

"Sure." Annabel sounded a bit surprised, but she slipped her little notebook over to Fran. "You want the pen as well?" It was one of her best metallic ones, a gorgeous silvery colour.

"No, I'll use pencil, then you can rub it out if you want." And Fran started to sketch round Annabel's stunning choker and tiara design.

"Oooh," murmured Becky, as she realized what Fran was drawing. "That's so cool! Which of us is it?"

Fran looked a bit embarrassed, and stared down at the pretty face she'd drawn in wearing Annabel's jewellery, which did look remarkably like one of the triplets. "All of you. Oops. Sorry, I know you hate it when people do that. I didn't think."

Becky grinned. "It's OK. We'll all be wearing the same for once on the wedding day – it'll be the first time in years. It'll be fun."

Annabel nodded and smiled too, but the smile hadn't quite got as far as her eyes, which were a little thoughtful. Did they really all have to look exactly the same? Couldn't their dresses be just a teensy bit different? She was sure there were ways she could improve on hers...

Then she leaned closer to Fran and added, "And if you give her a scowl it'll look absolutely spot-on for Katie..."

Mum and the triplets met Auntie Jan at Stallford station on Saturday morning, ready for a day of wedding shopping. Annabel could barely stand still for excitement, and Becky was bouncing on her toes, trying to see their aunt over the barrier. Even Katie seemed to have cheered up a bit – she really liked spending time with Auntie Jan. She wasn't trying to be dismal about the wedding, it was just that the idea of a whole day wearing clothes that were hard to walk in, and make-up that you could hardly talk in, in case it smudged, sounded awful. And it all seemed to take so long to organize. She liked dressing up occasionally, but her idea of dressing up was her nicest pair of velvet jeans and maybe just a tiny bit of Annabel's lipgloss. It did *not* involve curling irons, and there was no need for rosebuds whatsoever. It seemed stupid that Auntie Jan wanted the triplets to be a special part of her wedding, but they had to be super-perfect, unreal, china-doll girls, not the triplets themselves. Still, if that's what she wanted, Katie would do her best, even if she was secretly grinding her teeth the whole time. . .

"Auntie Jan!" Annabel had spotted their

aunt heading through the crowd, looking crisp and fresh and beautifully turned-out, as usual. They hugged all round, and headed off to a coffee shop nearby so that they could plan the day.

"So where's Mark today?" Mum asked, as she sipped her cappuccino, and the triplets tucked into milkshakes.

Auntie Jan took a mouthful of her jet-black espresso (which Becky thought looked like tar) and sighed happily. "Oh, he's on his stag do, didn't I tell you? He and his mates have gone to Silverstone for a motor-racing day – they get to drive the racing cars and everything. Sounds awful to me, but it's what he wanted. I just told his best man that I didn't mind as long as he came home in one piece and they didn't do anything crazy like shaving his eyebrows off." The triplets giggled, and Auntie Jan finished her coffee and pulled out a very organized-looking list. "OK. We're leaving the dresses till last, so we don't have to carry them around with us. And we need the florist, shoes, jewellery. . ."

Katie sighed – it was going to be a long day. . .

Becky reverently smoothed the dress–bag that was protecting her dress, and shut the wardrobe door carefully. The triplets shared a massive built–in wardrobe that filled one side of their bedroom. It was divided into three sections, one for each of them, but Annabel was currently using a good half of Katie's section as well as her own.

The dresses were now totally finished, and they looked fantastic. They'd had one last try–on in the shop to show Auntie Jan, with the dressmaker hovering worriedly in the background, in case anything was wrong, but their aunt had loved them, and she'd headed back to the station looking relieved. Now the dresses were to be stored away carefully until the big day. That was the plan, anyway. Katie had gratefully stuffed hers in the small section of wardrobe she could still get at, and disappeared off downstairs. Becky suspected that Annabel might have other ideas, from the thoughtful way she was eyeing the unzipped dress-bag lying on her bed.

She was right. Annabel was completely in love with her dress, and the idea of hiding it away for the next two weeks was torture. She didn't get a chance that day, but as soon as Becky and Katie were both well occupied downstairs on Sunday, she made a beeline for their bedroom and the dress.

She removed it gently from its bag and laid it carefully out on her bed to gloat. It was so lovely! She stroked the fabric gently, and gave the hem a thoughtful look. She'd really been hoping that when Auntie Jan saw the dresses yesterday she'd suddenly realize that there was something missing. The dresses just needed that extra bit of twinkle. But then Auntie Jan always wore very plain clothes, so she probably just hadn't spotted it, Annabel reasoned to herself. She wouldn't mind if Annabel added a little something, would she? And – Annabel suddenly grinned – this way, she would get to have a dress that was ever so slightly different from Katie and Becky's. She didn't have quite the same thing about identical clothes as Katie did, but it would be lovely to have an extra-special dress, one that was completely her own. She sat down next to the dress and started to plan. . .

Chapter Five

Once the dresses were safely put away (or hers was, anyway) Katie was able to forget about them for a while, and her mood improved. Mum had gone out with Max's dad again that Sunday evening, but she was being careful not to make the relationship too annoyingly obvious to the triplets, and they were doing their best to forget about it. A cheerful Katie made life a lot more fun, Becky thought to herself, watching her sister and the others all giggling over some silly joke as they waited for their English teacher to turn up on Monday. Maybe she could stop worrying about Katie, and just concentrate on enjoying the run-up to the wedding?

"Hey!" A hiss broke into her happy daydream. Becky sat up and looked over, and Katie and Annabel paused their discussion of who was the worst-dressed teacher in the school (current finalist, Mr Jones, their maths teacher, for his habit of wearing grey shoes).

Amy Mannering smiled sweetly at them, and Cara and Emily, her faithful followers, sniggered meaningfully.

Becky's heart sank. It would be so nice to have a day without Katie throwing a strop, or Max being vile, or this little lot trying to ruin things.

"What?" she snapped, far more forcefully than she would normally speak to Amy, who'd always scared her.

Amy blinked, not expecting a sharp answer from Becky, who she thought of as a total baby. But then she rallied. "So," she purred, "how are you getting on with your new big brother?"

Becky looked blank for a second, then realized that Amy must have picked up on the situation with Max. How did she *do* it? She was like a one-girl gossip column.

"So I suppose him and your new daddy will be moving in soon then?"

Katie looked as though she was about to leap up and throttle Amy right there in the classroom, but luckily Annabel broke in first.

"Oh shut up. How stupid can you be, Amy? Just shows how much you know about relationships, doesn't it?" She gave Amy one more dismissive, disgusted look, and turned back to the others, drawing Becky with her by the power of sisterly glare. Then she continued to talk, in a whisper that was calculated to carry as far as possible.

"I can't believe anyone could be that babyish, can you? I mean, I know Josh Matthews dumped her, but I thought she knew *something* about dating. So sad."

Much to Annabel's grim delight, Josh had indeed dumped Amy, only a week or so after the Valentine's Ball where she'd discovered them snuggled up together on a windowsill. The triplets hadn't been sure whether to be glad or sorry – as Annabel said, he and Amy deserved each other – but at least it wiped the triumphant smirk off Amy's face.

Even though Annabel had shut Amy up, the gloss had still gone from the day – the spectre of Max was back. And Becky had a horrible suspicion that Amy had been teasing him too – the triplets were her favourite prey, but she'd have a go at anybody she thought she could get at. Max was looking jumpy and upset – as though he might go off at the first person who annoyed him. Unfortunately, the triplets didn't actually have to *do* anything to annoy Max. At the moment, their very existence was enough to drive him mad, especially after Katie had humiliated him the week before. He'd recovered all his old nastiness, but he seemed to be even more desperate, and more hurtful. Katie was his main target – he was aching to pay her back – but he was ready to attack any of the triplets, or their gang of friends. He spent a good ten minutes of their French class that afternoon chucking little balls of paper over at their table, which all turned out to have horrible comments written on them. That just showed how desperate he was, as Mr Hatton, their French teacher, was the strictest person on the planet, and practically telepathic about people messing around in his lessons. Max was lucky, though – Mr Hatton must have been having an off-day. Either that or he was too fascinated by irregular verbs to spot Max's tricks.

Becky was really relieved to get home that afternoon – she wanted some time to relax, safely away from Max and Amy and all the stress of school. Mum had a rush project on at the moment, so she greeted the triplets with her hair all on end, and a request to make toast to tide them over for a bit, and she'd get on with tea as soon as she'd got a bit more done. Becky wasn't feeling particularly hungry, so she nipped upstairs to dump her school bag and get changed, and say hello to Cassie and Fang, then she headed out to the garden shed to spend some quality time with the guinea pigs.

After twenty minutes of soothing squeaks, peanut-nibbling and soft fur, she was feeling a lot better. She almost felt ready to face her French homework, which was really saying something. She passed Katie up at the top of the garden, where there was a clear space that she used for football practice. She wasn't looking as though she wanted to talk, but was glaring grimly at the ball, as though daring it not to do what she wanted. Max had really got to her.

Annabel was in the kitchen, helping Mum make dinner – Mum was looking a lot more human, and humming happily as she chopped the vegetables.

Becky headed upstairs, and found Orlando and Pixie on the landing, looking ve-e-ery smug for some reason. Becky looked at them suspiciously. They didn't always get on, so it was quite rare to see them sitting so cosily together. They gazed back at her innocently, and Orlando licked his lips and gave a luxurious stretch.

The triplets' bedroom door was open, which was annoying, as everyone was supposed to keep it shut to make sure the cats didn't get in. They were quite capable of frightening the rats to death by prowling round the cage, or if they worked together they could probably knock it over. If they worked together! Oh no! Becky looked back at the cats' smug faces, and quickened her pace up the stairs towards the open door. She was dreading what she would find as she rushed into the bedroom.

The cage door was hanging open. Becky's heart seemed to jump into her mouth and she gave a little squawk of horror. She scanned the floor desperately – no sad small furry heaps. But what if the cats had eaten . . . *everything!*

She felt sick, but she forced herself to search the room methodically; under all the beds, everywhere. Nothing. She'd been leaving the cage till last. She didn't want to see the evidence of the cats' attack – the broken door, rat toys and bedding spilt everywhere.

Finally she couldn't put it off any longer, and she crept over to the windowseat. Strangely, the cage door seemed to be fine – it was just open. And the cage looked as tidy as a cage full of rats ever looks. In fact, that was what it was – a cage full of rats. Becky stared in amazement at Cassie and Fang, snoozing blissfully in their nest, whiskers whiffling gently as they breathed in and out. They were both very much alive.

Becky took what seemed like the first full breath she'd had in ages, shut the cage door with trembling fingers and then sat down suddenly on the windowseat beside them. She couldn't believe it. She must not have closed the cage properly when she'd come up to say hi to the rats earlier, and it had swung open. She was amazed that the rats hadn't made a bid for freedom, though. They loved to run about on the floor. The problem normally was stopping them invading Annabel's declared rat-free zone. Becky had to build book barricades to keep them where they were allowed to be, and that was almost useless anyway, as they were such fantastic climbers. Becky shook her head slowly as she stared down into the cage.

Then suddenly she leaned forward. Just what were Cassie and Fang sleeping on? That was not their normal bed of chewed-up paper – it was shiny. *Satiny,* in fact. Yes, their nest was flecked with scraps of soft, white, satiny fabric.

Becky froze. Then she turned round very slowly, and looked over at Annabel's bed. Uh-huh. Her sister had been trying on the bridesmaid's dress again, and left it lying spread out on her bed, the hem trailing very slightly on the floor – almost as though it had been pulled there by little rat claws. Becky got up, and walked jerkily over to the dress. It was still beautiful. In fact, the delicate pattern of lacy holes around the hem of the front panel really added something, she told herself frantically. She just wasn't sure that Annabel, or – an even worse thought – Auntie Jan, were going to agree. . .

Becky panicked. What was she going to do? Annabel was going to kill her, and then the rats – or possibly the other way round. Becky's mind was jumping desperately around, willing it not to be true, searching for some magical solution.

"Becky!"

She jumped, and yelped in horror. That was Annabel! Was she coming upstairs? What should she do? She snatched up the dress and clutched it to her, hiding the chewed side.

"Becky! Tea-ea!"

Oh. It was OK – for the moment. Annabel

was just standing at the bottom of the stairs to call her down.

Becky licked her lips nervously, and managed to croak, "Coming."

She heard Annabel bouncing back into the kitchen.

There was no time for any clever ideas right now, but Becky couldn't just leave the dress. Annabel would be back to put it away later, and she'd be bound to spot the holes. Becky quickly stuffed the dress back into its bag, and put it away – in her bit of the wardrobe. Fingers slipping with nervousness, she took her own dress, unzipped the bag, and laid the satiny creation gently on Annabel's bed, as close as she could to where she guessed the original had been.

Then, still trembling, she went downstairs to force down some food.

Chapter Six

Now that she'd added the pattern of twinkly beads round the hem of her bridesmaid's dress, Annabel was even more in love with it than before. It was partly her own work now, which made it so much better. Of course, it meant that she wanted to try it on even more often. On Tuesday evening, after a trying day at school, she headed upstairs for a spot of dress therapy. All of their teachers seemed to have had the sole aim of making everyone's lives miserable by loading them with homework, and Max Cooper had spent the entire day hissing mean comments at the triplets. Not that Annabel really let Max get to her – she didn't intend to, anyway – but the constant drip-drip-drip of nastiness was quite depressing. Even Becky had started to doubt her nice ideas about making friends with such a monster.

Annabel had been curled up on the stairs, trying to force her brain to understand the periodic table, when she'd decided enough was enough. She'd even tried her patented (well, it would be if she knew how) method for when homework was particularly impossible. She would reverse her normal position, so that instead of facing up the stairs, she was facing down, with her books on the third step, elbows on the fourth and so on. It was supposed to send the blood to her brain, but it had proved absolutely useless in the face of the noble gases. Honestly! Why did anyone need to know this stuff? She shoved all her books and bits to the side of the stairs – Mum had got sick of tripping over her pencil case – and made for their bedroom. Katie and Becky were sitting at the big table looking as though the periodic table was taking its toll on them too. Actually, Becky had been looking funny all day, and Annabel had assumed it was because Max was really getting to her. She even looked as though she hadn't slept properly; all white, and shadowy eyes. Drat Max! Annabel resolved to work out some really choice insults ready for tomorrow, so she could leap in and reduce him to a puddle of quivering jelly if he so much as looked at Becky. The dress would probably inspire her, and she was pretty sure Katie and Becky wouldn't notice what she'd done – it was quite subtle, and they were concentrating. She smiled to herself as she lifted the dress-bag out of the wardrobe.

Meanwhile, Becky had flinched as she saw Annabel come in, and was now watching miserably as her sister got out the dress – her dress. What *was* she going to do? It was less than two weeks to the wedding, and she hadn't got even the merest wisp of a plan. She had a little bit of money in her bank account – maybe she could get it out and somehow sneak off to the dressmaker with Bel's dress and beg her to mend the chewed bits? But she had a horrible feeling that the dressmaker would ring Mum as soon as she walked in the door.

Annabel's happy expression as she lifted out the dress was torture. Becky sighed, which caught Annabel's attention. She smiled sympathetically. "Max has got to you too? Look, come and try your dress on – it'll cheer you up, honestly!"

Becky shuddered, and shook her head. She muttered something about homework and turned back to the table.

Annabel stroked the smooth folds of the dress, and admired the crystal beads she'd sewn on so carefully – or would have done, except they weren't there. She gave the dress a puzzled look, and then her face cleared. Somehow her dress had got mixed up with one of the other two. Perhaps Becky had been trying hers on again too! She flicked a glance quickly round at her sisters – Katie was working away, and Becky was now staring hard at the table, probably pondering a difficult question. She didn't really want it to be too obvious that she was putting this dress back – after all, the three dresses were supposed to be absolutely identical, so how would she know this one wasn't hers? Even though she'd convinced herself it was OK to make her dress different, she wasn't sure what Katie and Becky's reactions to the added extras would be. Quickly she found the dress-bag in Becky's wardrobe and pulled it out, not noticing that Becky was now gazing at her in horror.

Annabel had got as far as undoing the zip, before Becky managed to find her tongue. "Wh-what are you doing?" she quavered.

Annabel jumped, and nearly dropped the dress, and Katie turned round curiously. "I'm just going to try the dress on again, that's all!" Annabel blustered.

"But that's Becky's dress," Katie pointed out – she could see that it was Becky's wardrobe door that was open.

Annabel shrugged, and tried to brazen it out. "I think they got mixed up," she murmured vaguely, hoping that Katie would just shut up and go back to her homework. She shouldn't have tried to do this with the other two in the room, she told herself crossly. Well, the worst that could happen was Katie had a go at her for trying to make her dress more special – and in Katie's current mood she wouldn't care anyway! This thought trailed off as Annabel drew out the dress and caught sight of the chewed skirt. She gasped sharply.

"What's the matter?" asked Katie, getting up to look. Becky was glued to her chair, watching in panic as the whole disaster began to unfold.

"Beckyyyy!" Annabel snarled. It was obvious that this was something to do with Becky – the dress had been in her wardrobe, and she was looking unbelievably guilty. Annabel wasn't an animal expert, but those holes looked like chewing, and that had to be Becky's fault. She flung the dress on to her bed and marched over to her sister, who shrank back in her chair, gazing up at her like a rabbit caught in headlights.

"What happened to my dress! It was those disgusting little beasts, wasn't it?"

She veered off and headed for the rat cage, looking as though she wanted to strangle one of them. That got Becky out of her chair faster than anything else could have done. She whizzed across the room and stood in front of the cage, fending Annabel off.

"It wasn't their fault! Don't touch them! Annabel, *please!*"

"I said I didn't want them in our room! I said it would be a disaster, and now look what they've done!" Annabel's voice rose to a wail as she pointed at the ruined dress.

Katie peered over. "Oh wow. Oh no – the

rats did this?" She turned a horror-struck face to Becky.

"I'm really sorry, Bel!" Becky had realized that the rats were no longer in immediate danger from Annabel, who was practically in tears now as she knelt in front of the dress and fingered the damage, and she came over to look at it with the other two. "I must have left the cage open by accident, and the dress was lying on your bed – they – they –" She trailed off, realizing that Annabel probably wouldn't react well to any more rat info. But it was too late.

"They what?" Annabel snapped.

"They made a nest out of it. . ." whispered Becky, and Annabel wailed again.

"When was this?" Katie asked, getting straight to the point.

"Yesterday. I didn't know what to do, so I just swapped Bel's dress with mine while I tried to think of a plan."

Annabel glared at her. "Well, I think that's a very good plan. You can wear the horrible *chewed-up* dress to the wedding, and I'll wear yours! And those rats can go and live in the garden shed where they should have been in the first place!"

Becky's face crumpled. Of course, it was perfectly fair that she should wear the rat-eaten dress, but somehow she'd managed to blank out the reality of one of them having to wear it – and that it was ruined because of her. Now it was obvious that she was going to be the one to spoil Auntie Jan's wedding. And she'd done all that worrying about Katie!

Katie looked at her two sisters, now both crying, and sighed resignedly. No use expecting any help from *them* then. She picked up the dress, and held it out in front of her critically. Stupid thing. Oh, she could see that it was very pretty, but she and "very pretty" just didn't really get on. Still – now that something awful had happened to one of the dresses, she was feeling a bit guilty. After all, this was exactly what she'd been wishing for.

Now she'd got it, she was realizing that however much she didn't want to wear a satiny meringue, she wanted the wedding to go beautifully for Auntie Jan even more. It was time somebody *did* something, instead of sitting on the floor crying. Unfortunately, that was as far as she could get – she had no idea what you did with a dress full of holes.

"Oh, stop crying, you two! It won't help. You shouldn't have let the rats get out, Becky, and you shouldn't have left your dress on the bed, Bel. It's both your faults, and now we're just going to have to sort it out."

Streaming tears, Becky looked up at the dress as Katie held it out, still considering the damage. "That – that dress has got – beads on it," she hiccupped.

Katie looked at them. "Uh–huh." She looked at Becky. "And?"

"Well, it – shouldn't have."

"Oh. I see what you mean. The others don't?"

Becky shook her head, and gazed at Annabel.

"I put the beads on because I wanted it to be sparkly," Annabel sniffed. "It took ages, and now it's sparkly with holes!"

Katie rolled her eyes – as if a meringue wasn't enough. "So you sewed these on?" she said thoughtfully. "Have you got more?"

"Some." Annabel was sitting up straighter now, looking consideringly at the dress. "And Saima's got loads. She was with me when we bought them in the craft shop in town."

"So, can you mend it? Add more beads somehow?"

"I don't see how," moaned Annabel, slumping back down again. "It's still got holes in – adding beads won't stop that."

Becky suddenly jumped up, and headed for the door. "Wait for me a minute," she called back over her shoulder, leaving the other two staring after her, not sure whether to feel hopeful or not.

She came back waving a copy of *Brides*

magazine. "Look! I just remembered when you said about the beads not filling in the holes, Bel. Auntie Jan was looking at this dress, and said she thought it was really pretty, but not her style. But that doesn't mean *we* couldn't do it."

She pointed to a picture of a wedding dress, modelled by an impossibly tall girl with perfectly upswept hair and the whitest teeth ever.

"Look at the design round the skirt!" The long creamy-white dress had a decoration of shimmery gold beads that formed a lacework around the hem.

Annabel looked at it critically. "It's a bit cutesy – those little heart shapes."

Becky decided not to comment on this opinion from someone who was wearing heart-shaped earrings, heart hairclips and very probably had hearts printed on her knickers.

"Yes, so we'd do it better! I thought when I

saw what Cassie and Fang had done that it was almost like lace. . ." She shut up. Annabel's face was saying very clearly that she did not want to hear about the lace-making abilities of rats, and Becky really didn't want to remind her sister they existed – she might remember her demand for them to be exiled to the shed.

But Annabel, for the moment, was more concerned with the beading plan. She picked up the magazine and studied the picture carefully, looking from it to the dress and back again. "It might work," she said dubiously.

Katie looked over her shoulder. "It would be pretty obvious, wouldn't it. I mean, everyone would notice that this dress was different to the other two."

"It's already got beads on," Becky argued. "This would just be more."

But Annabel was nodding. "I only put a few on before – I just thought it would make it a teensy bit different, not that people would

really notice. You couldn't not notice that."
She pointed to the photo.

Becky's eyes filled with tears all over again.
It had seemed such a good idea!

"I'm not saying we shouldn't do it," said
Katie slowly. "I'm saying we'd have to do the
other two dresses as well."

The others looked at her in shock.

"What, change them on purpose?"
whispered Becky.

"Mmm. If you think we can do it well
enough, Bel. 'Cause otherwise we're going to
have to go to Mum and tell her that this dress
needs to go back to the dressmaker and have
half a new skirt put on it. And from the look on
her face when she found out how much they
were going to cost in the first place, I don't
think she'd be very happy."

Becky flinched, and Annabel looked serious
for once. That was true. What with the dresses,
and shoes and jewellery and everything else,
the wedding was costing a lot, and Mum was

helping out Auntie Jan with loads of stuff, so she was stressed and busy anyway, plus there was all the work she was trying to cram in.

All three of them realized at the same time that Mum was probably working so hard because she was trying to make some extra money to pay for the dresses. They exchanged worried looks, and then decisive ones. They were going to sort this out themselves, without upsetting Mum any more.

Annabel whipped out her mobile. "We're going to need help. Sorry to be mean, Katie, but you can't sew. We need people who can – and we need somewhere we can do this without Mum walking in and going ballistic. I'm calling Saima, OK?"

Katie and Becky nodded fervently. Saima was almost as much of a fashion goddess as Annabel, and she had a huge loft-conversion bedroom that would be perfect for turning into a dress workshop.

Annabel called, and quickly explained the

situation to Saima. Katie and Becky could hear the horrified exclamations as Saima heard the fate of the dress. She seemed to be up for helping out, though.

"Uh-huh. Uh-huh. Oh yes, good idea! Yes, go and ask." Annabel looked over at Becky and Katie. "Saima's suggesting we have a sleepover on Saturday at her house, and we'll invite the others too. That way we've got a chance of getting all three dresses done. Hi! It's OK? Excellent. Yeah, we'll go and ask our mum, but I'm sure it'll be OK. We're not doing anything this weekend."

That was what Annabel thought, but when the triplets surged downstairs to tackle Mum, she was surprisingly doubtful.

"Oh. Well, I don't know. . ."

"Why not, Mum?" asked Becky, sounding panicky – surely this last chance wasn't going to be snatched away? "We've done all the wedding stuff, haven't we?"

"Ye-es," Mum agreed hesitantly. "But I

wanted to talk to you – we've had an invitation for Sunday." She was trying to sound upbeat, but the girls could tell from her voice that she was worried about how they were going to react to her news. They frowned at her. What was going on?

"Jeff – Max's dad – has asked us all over for Sunday lunch."

The three identical frowns deepened as the triplets digested this. Even Becky wasn't feeling very charitable to Max right now. After all, it was his fault all of this had happened! If she hadn't been feeling so stressed out by him she'd never have left the rat cage open.

Mum continued, with the air of someone who knows there's a fierce wild animal (or three fierce wild animals) close behind them, and is trying very hard not to run however much they want to. "And I said that would be lovely."

There was a meaningful silence. Finally Annabel said, "But that's on Sunday. We can be back from Saima's in time to go to lunch – if we have to."

Katie took a deep breath. It looked like not making a fuss about the lunch at Max's house could be the only way to get the dresses sorted. She noted Becky's pleading stare, and nodded. "Exactly. Please, Mum! We'll be back in loads of time."

"Oh, OK then," Mum sounded relieved – as though she'd expected a fight, and was happy to compromise. "You'll have to do all your homework on Saturday before you go, though."

"Uh-huh!" That was Becky, as she whisked out of the kitchen door, chasing the other two up the stairs. They needed to have a crisis meeting!

Chapter Seven

Max had obviously been told about the lunch too, because he got worse and worse all week. He was in detention twice for disrupting classes while he tried to upset the triplets – pulling Katie's hair, deliberately knocking all Becky's stuff on to the floor. Normally the weekend would at least have been a rest from him, but now they had to go and have quality time with him and his dad! Katie was furious, and had a real go at him in the playground on Friday. What really worried Becky though, was that the look of malicious glee, which used to terrify her when Max was being awful, had gone entirely. Instead Max looked desperate – as though he knew he was fighting with his back against a wall. She was still certain that because he didn't have his mum, the relationship between their parents was going to be harder for him than it was for her and Katie and Annabel, and she still felt sorry for him – though she tended to forget that when he was tripping her up in the corridor on the way to geography.

"You did that on purpose!" Katie yelled, squaring up to Max as Annabel and the others hurried to pick Becky up. "I can't believe you, you're mad! You could have really hurt her!"

"Oh, don't be such a baby!" scoffed Max, although he did peer round at Becky a little anxiously, to see if she was hurt enough to get him into trouble. She looked shaken but mostly OK, so he decided to make a quick getaway. When the girls arrived in geography he was sitting there with all his books out, looking as though butter wouldn't melt. Katie seethed through the rest of the day – even though it had been Becky Max had tripped, she was still taking it as a personal insult. It was becoming obvious that Sunday was going to be torture.

What made it even worse was that Mum was so excited about it. Becky had seen her trying on outfits in front of the mirror and humming to herself, and she kept making cheerful little references to Sunday. She was going to get a big shock when she saw Katie and Max in the same room together – it was going to be awful. Becky decided she needed advice. She hated arguments so much, and she really wanted Sunday not to be a total disaster, for Mum's sake if nothing else.

She headed up to the loft that evening to email Dad. It might seem funny to talk, to him about problems with Mum's new boyfriend, but after the first months of awfulness, her parents' split had left them on reasonably good terms. Becky knew Dad would be happy that Mum was meeting new people.

She opened up her email account and tried to think what to say. This was going to take some explaining – for a start because she still didn't know how she felt about the whole thing.

After half an hour of typing and deleting and more typing and deleting again, Becky sighed as she hit "send". It felt better having moaned thoroughly to somebody – but it wasn't as if Dad could actually do much to help.

By standing over her armed with a maths textbook, Katie had managed to get Annabel to finish all her homework in time for the sleepover at Saima's. Now they just had to find a way to get the three dresses in the car without Mum realizing what was going on. Katie wanted to roll them up inside their sleeping bags, but Annabel nearly had a fit at this. In the end they had to resort to the time-honoured ploy of one triplet as the distraction while the other two got on with whatever it was they weren't supposed to be doing. This was one of those times when being a threesome got really useful.

The triplets had stowed all their stuff in the

car, and were just grabbing their jackets –
Mum insisted they took them – when Annabel
suddenly screamed.

Mum jumped and dropped the car keys.
"What? What?"

"There's a *massive* spider, there on the
ceiling!"

There *was* a spider, but only because Katie
had gone out in the garden and caught it and
put it there on purpose. Annabel was well
known to be terrified of spiders – the plan had
involved great personal sacrifice on her part,
and she'd had to be towed through the hall
with her eyes closed by the other two ever since
the long-legged creature had been put in place.

"Oh my goodness," said Mum faintly,
looking at the spider. "So there is. Well. It's
quite big, isn't it. . ."

Annabel had inherited her terror of spiders
from Mum, but Mum always tried incredibly
hard to pretend she didn't mind them. It didn't
work.

Katie smiled. "Would you like me to get it down, Mum? Can you help me get the stepladder out?"

"Oh! Oh yes, that would be very helpful, Katie, thank you." Mum dived through the kitchen door, where she was safely out of sight of the horrible thing, and headed for the big cupboard by the back door. Katie beetled after her, signalling at the other two – go, go, go!

Becky and Annabel dashed upstairs for the dresses and hid them in the boot of the car just in time. Katie captured the spider in a jam jar and took it back out to the garden to set it free. By now it was feeling deeply confused, and it scuttled under the fence to next door, where it was hoping for a quieter life.

The triplets were pretty sure that when they got to Saima's house, Mum would go and have a cup of tea with Saima's parents and let them unload the car, and luckily they were right. They whisked the dresses up to Saima's bedroom before anyone could spot what was going on. Saima was bouncing about excitedly. She'd got out all her beads, and her sewing stuff, and loads of bits she'd borrowed from her mum, who was brilliant at making clothes. The best thing was that Saima's mum had a dressmaker's dummy, a sort of body on a stand that you could use to fit dresses on. That would be very helpful for hanging the dresses on while they worked out the bead decoration.

Saima drew in her breath in horror when she saw the rat-chewed dress. "Oh no! Look at it." She drew the skirt out and surveyed the damage, shaking her head. "I didn't realize it would be this bad," she confessed to Annabel. "But I'm sure we can sort it," she added, seeing her friend's panicked face.

"I could kill those rats," Annabel muttered furiously, shooting a glare at Becky. Only the knowledge (drummed into her by Katie) that it was partly her own fault for leaving the dress out on her bed, which they'd been forbidden to do, was stopping Annabel from demanding that Becky move the rats out to the garden shed to live with the guinea pigs. But she still kept making nasty comments about traps and poison all the time.

When Fran and Megan had arrived, Saima and Annabel called a strategy meeting. The rat-customized dress was on the dressmaker's dummy and Annabel stared glumly at it. "OK. You all know the situation. We've got three dresses, and we need to turn them into something like this." She brandished the page from the wedding magazine.

Fran peered over at it. "Can I see?" She held out a hand. "This is really nice! Have you got everything we need?"

Saima held out a shoebox that was full of little pots and packets of beads.

"Wow! Saima, these are beautiful. You've got all these different purpley ones, and some silver. You could do a fantastic design with these."

Fran's enthusiasm seemed to rub off on Annabel and Saima, and they went into a huddle with a sketchbook, drawing out various patterns, and trying to fit them to the shape the rats had already mapped out on the dress. Annabel had brought tracing paper, and eventually they came up with a spray of flowers and leaves that they all agreed on.

"And the best thing is," Saima said excitedly, "that it actually looks better in that random sort of scatter that the rats made. If we'd tried to do it ourselves I don't think it would be as good. And you wanted beads in the first place. Those rats have done you a favour, Bel!"

Annabel sniffed. She was never going to admit *that.* But the design was looking great – now it was just a case of sewing it, and finding out whether they were good enough to make it work. . .

Becky, Katie and Megan had been sitting watching. As none of them were hugely artistic, they hadn't felt like they could add much – they were there to be the slave labour.

"OK!" Annabel stood up. "Me and Saima will sew the beads on my dress, 'cause that's the most complicated one with all the *chewed bits*." Here she glared at Becky. "We need to stop it fraying any more. Becky and Fran will do her dress, and then when we've finished we'll all do your dress, Katie."

"What do we do?" asked Katie, sounding slightly hurt. OK, so she couldn't sew to save her life, and nor could Megan, but they wanted to do *something*.

Annabel grinned at her. "This is where being boringly good at maths comes in useful for once. You two can sort the beads out for us. Look," she handed over the original flower design, "these are silver, these are violet – you see? All the colours are marked on. You need to put the right beads for each bit in these little bowls."

Katie nodded briskly. *That* she could do.

Everyone got to work. Saima had a really cool sound system, and she put some music on to liven things up. Luckily her parents had promised to stay out of the way, as long as they went to bed at a "reasonable" time.

Becky and Fran started the ticklish job of sewing on the beads, one by one, following the pattern. It was difficult, but fun – and they did look very pretty.

After half an hour or so, Annabel got up and stretched. "Oof! I've got a crick in my neck. How's yours going, Becky?" She peered over. "That looks nice – but hey, hang on, that flower's meant to be the lilac colour, not the crystal! You'll have to undo it."

Becky looked horrified – that flower had taken ages – but Fran gazed at the dress thoughtfully, and then over at Annabel's. She shook her head. "I'm not sure, Bel. I think it would be better if they weren't exactly the same – I mean, obviously it's going to be the same basic design, but I don't see why each petal has to be the same. What's the point of hand-decorating the dresses if they still look like a machine did them?"

Annabel looked slightly gobsmacked. Fran was so easygoing that she didn't often disagree – but Annabel could see she was right.

Becky grinned at her. "And that's what you wanted in the first place, Bel," she pointed out. "A dress that was just the teensiest bit different."

Annabel pulled a face at her, but went back to her own dress with no more argument.

The sewing took a great deal longer than the sorting out of all the beads, and so Katie and Megan were at a loose end fairly quickly. They unrolled their sleeping bags in an out-of-the-way corner, and settled down to chat with everybody.

"I can't believe we've got to go to lunch with Max tomorrow," Katie grumbled. "He's such a little monster, and he's just getting meaner and meaner."

Becky sighed. Why couldn't Katie see it? Max was only getting meaner because he was miserable. She decided to have one more go at explaining this. She'd read Dad's reply to her complaining email before they came out, and he'd been really sympathetic. He told her that Katie and Bel had been moaning about it too, and as far as he could see, the only way forward was what she was already trying – getting Katie and Max to understand each other a bit more.

"I reckon he's only being a pain because he's scared," she said timidly.

Katie grinned evilly. "Good. The more scared the better."

"Don't be horrible!" protested Becky. "You don't really mean that."

"I do," replied Katie firmly. "He's a pig and I can't stand him. And stop trying to make everything nice, Becky, it won't work. It's your fault that I have to go tomorrow, because if it hadn't been for needing to sort the dresses out

I would've said no." And she turned over pointedly to talk to Megan.

Everyone looked a bit surprised at Katie's sharpness, and Fran gave Becky a sympathetic look. Becky just stared back at her, lost for words. She'd tried her best with Katie. What else could she do?

The dresses were eventually finished well after midnight, and they looked fantastic – even Annabel was pleased with the way they'd turned out. The girls crawled into their sleeping bags, exhausted, but triumphant – surely even Auntie Jan would like them?

Chapter Eight

Becky didn't think she'd ever been on quite such a silent car journey. Mum was too nervous to talk. She just kept tapping her fingernails on the steering wheel every time they had to stop at lights. She'd been like it ever since she picked the triplets up from Saima's, which had luckily meant that she was far too jittery to notice them sneaking the newly customized dresses back into the car. Apart from the slightly manic body-language, she was looking very good – wearing the cardigan and scarf that the triplets had got her for Christmas, but with jeans. Annabel approved – Mum was going for casual but nice, like she hadn't made too much of an effort. It was just a pity that a) they'd seen the mound of clothes on her bed and knew it had probably taken her about three hours to get that thrown-together look, and b) she was doing it all for Max's dad.

Mum had looked thoughtfully at the three of them when they came downstairs from putting all their stuff away and getting changed, and got as far as opening her mouth to say something before deciding it wasn't a good idea. Becky was fairly sure that what she'd wanted to say was that it would be nice if Katie could have made a bit more of an effort, and did Annabel really have to wear a skirt that short. She herself was wearing a purple flounced cord skirt and a gypsy-ish sort of top, and she didn't think Mum could find that much to disapprove of. Katie and Annabel were both looking so mulish that most people wouldn't get past the sulky expressions on their faces to notice the clothes anyway. The reality of Mum and Mr Cooper seemed to have made Annabel just as grumpy as Katie, now that she didn't have the dress drama to distract her any more.

When Mum finally pulled up outside Max's house, everyone sat looking at it for a few seconds before making any move to get out of the car. Then Mum turned a too-cheerful smile on them and chirped, "Come on then!" No one moved. "Look, girls, I know you're not happy about this – but I'm sure it will work out. Really."

They looked narrowly at her, even Becky, who was desperately trying to go along with this for her sake, and Mum deflated slightly, and made a big thing about getting out of the car and finding her bag. Then she looked back at them. The triplets huddled together, feeling the need for some sisterly backing-up, as Mum rang the doorbell.

Becky was convinced she could hear some angry, loud "whispering" on the other side of the door that was Max's dad trying to get him to open the door and be polite, but it obviously didn't work because Mr Cooper opened the door himself, and the triplets could see Max scowling in the kitchen doorway, looking disgusted at his dad's hearty welcome.

"Right! Come on in and have a drink! Girls! Lemonade? Coke? Juice?" Max's dad was obviously very nervous too – he was waving his arms around like a mad waiter.

"Lemonade, please," said Becky politely, and got death – stared by Katie, Annabel *and* Max. She wilted slightly. What was so wrong with just wanting people to get along?

"Something smells nice!" commented Mrs Ryan, still sounding hyper-cheerful.

Max muttered something that Becky reckoned was probably very rude, but luckily no one could really hear it.

"Oh good, it's my speciality, chicken casserole." Max's dad seized on this lifeline with both hands and yammered on about the recipe for ages, while Max and the girls sulked as far away from each other as they could possibly get in a reasonably sized kitchen.

The Coopers had a big corkboard on the kitchen wall, covered in letters from school, useful phone numbers, that kind of thing. The triplets were right next to it, and they couldn't help noticing a distinctly familiar piece of card. A wedding invitation. Auntie Jan's wedding invitation, to be precise. . .

"Mum!" Katie interrupted Max's dad in the middle of his description of precisely how he'd chopped the courgettes. "Why've *they* got a wedding invitation?"

"Don't be so rude, Katie!" said her mum, sounding flustered.

Mr Cooper smiled hugely at Katie and said in a very enthusiastic voice, "Your aunt was kind enough to send Max and me an invitation, Annabel. We're looking forward to it. I gather we get to see you three as bridesmaids?"

Katie looked at him, contempt practically dripping off her. "*This* is Annabel. I'm Katie."

"Oh! Oh dear, sorry – you're all so alike."

Annabel had kept sight of the important point. "You mean, *he* is coming to Auntie Jan's wedding?" she asked, flicking her curls at Max.

"Not if you still want me to be a bridesmaid, he's not," stated Katie, folding her arms and looking at Mum with a stone-like expression. "I put up with all this dress stuff, fittings and that sort of rubbish, but I'm not having *him* anywhere near me."

"Well, I wouldn't come if you paid me, anyway!" snarled Max, facing up to her. "Why would I want to spend a day with you and your stupid mother and your stupid family?"

"Max! I can't believe you just said that – apologize, now!"

Mr Cooper's voice was so scary that Becky wasn't surprised when Max muttered, "Sorry," immediately, and then slunk out when his dad told him to get out of his sight.

Mrs Ryan was looking white with embarrassment. "I'm so sorry. Katie, I'm ashamed of you – what makes you think you have any say in who comes to the wedding? You're all three being bridesmaids, and there's no question about it. It's an honour to have been asked, and you will go, and you will behave *beautifully*, whoever is there to see you. Is that clear?"

Katie said nothing, just kept up her stony stare.

"I asked you a question, Katie!" Mum snapped, sounding as though she might be about to lose it entirely, and Katie snarled, "Yes," in a voice that was scarcely less furious.

There was an uncomfortable silence, and then Mr Cooper suggested, sounding slightly desperate, "Um, why don't we all go and sit down? The food should all be ready, I think."

He ushered them anxiously from the kitchen into the dining room, and muttered something about giving Max a bit more time to cool off.

The tense situation had made Becky down

her lemonade, just for something to do, and now she was desperate for the loo. She nudged Mum, not wanting to ask herself. Mum looked irritably at her. "Jeff, could you tell Becky where the loo is?"

"Yes, of course, sorry!" It looked like anything could fluster Max's dad right now. "Just out of here, into the hall, and it's under the stairs."

"Thanks." Becky escaped gratefully, wondering how long it was reasonable to be in the loo for, and how many times you could go in one meal.

She bolted out into the hall, and headed for the stairs – but then she was stopped in her tracks. She could hear a murmuring, whining noise. Was it Max's cute little Jack Russell? She hadn't seen him yet, which was odd. Suddenly she really wanted to spend some time with something sensible and lovely, like a dog, instead of all these warring people. Maybe he was shut in upstairs – it wouldn't matter if she had a quick peep, would it?

She crept quietly up the first level of the stairs – it was a tall old house, and there looked to be lots of them. Suddenly, the whining noise was replaced with another, a low voice talking. Becky shrank into the wall, scared to be discovered where she had no right to be. But the owner of the voice wasn't coming down. It was Max, and he was sitting halfway up the next flight of stairs, with the little dog on his lap. Becky peered up carefully – she could just about see through the banisters. Max was leaning over, hugging the dog tight, and muttering into his ear, rocking them both backwards and forwards a little. The dog was whining anxiously, and licking the boy's face, as though it was worried about him.

"It isn't fair! You know, don't you, Lucky? He's forgotten all about her. How could he? It's like she never existed. How could he even think about going out with somebody else? We've got to stop it, Lucky. You were Mum's dog, you don't want anyone else around, do you? Maybe you can bite them all for me, hey?" He sniffed, and Becky wondered whether he was crying. She felt guilty, eavesdropping like this, but it certainly explained a lot about Max. She'd been right – he was furious that his dad was trying to replace his mum.

She realized that she'd better get back. She sneaked quickly down the stairs, and found the loo – which had sweet Jack Russell pictures in it, probably bought by Max's mum.

Back in the dining room the atmosphere hadn't improved much. Mum gave her a "where have you been?" glare, backed up by matching ones from Katie and Annabel.

It was a tortuous meal. Once he'd got all the food on the table – and he must have been cooking all week as there was enough to feed the whole of their class, practically – Mr Cooper went and fetched Max, who came down with Lucky. Thankfully, it was a big dining table, and he didn't have to sit close to any of the triplets. It was Ryans at one end, and Coopers at the other.

No one ate very much. Max just fed titbits to Lucky under the table, and the tiny dog probably ate as much as all the people sitting above him put together. When Mr Cooper realized that he really wasn't going to be able to force seconds down anyone, he dragged Max off into the kitchen to help him get the pudding ready. It was pretty obvious that this was an excuse to try and beg Max to behave – or that his dad had realized that it wasn't a good idea to leave him alone with the Ryans. . .

The triplets' mum grabbed the same opportunity.

"What on earth is the matter with you three? You're behaving terribly, and Jeff is trying so hard to be nice!"

All three triplets glared at her – even Becky didn't see how her mum could be so stupid. Mrs Ryan looked at their set, angry faces – especially Katie's – and then sighed and looked away, as though she'd made some sort of decision, not one she was happy about.

When Max and his dad came back, carrying a massive dish of apple crumble and a jug of custard, she smiled rather sadly at them. "That looks lovely. Why don't you four all have some. Jeff, do you think we could have a word?"

Mr Cooper nodded, grimly. He didn't seem at all surprised. They went back into the kitchen together. Surprisingly, because neither parent had made dire threats about being nice to each other or else, Max and the triplets felt a bit at a loss. They didn't eat the apple crumble, but they didn't throw it at each other either. They just sat and strained their ears to hear what was going on in the kitchen. It was hard to work out what was happening – a very serious conversation by the sound of it. But Becky had a horrible feeling that she knew what they were saying, and Mum's face when she and Jeff came back in told her she'd been right.

"Oh! You didn't have any pudding. Oh dear.

I'm sorry, you three, but we've got to go."

The triplets jumped up eagerly, desperate to be out of there. Mum seemed to feel the same way, rushing them into their coats and shepherding them out to the car – as though she didn't want to give herself a chance to change her mind.

They were halfway home when she made a little coughing noise, and then said. "Jeff and I have decided not to see each other any more at the moment. After what happened at lunch – well, it's just not going to work, is it?" She smiled sadly.

The triplets waited for more, but that was all Mum said, and when they got home she went up to her room and stayed there and Becky was sure that she could hear her crying.

Chapter Nine

Becky decided, right there on the landing, that enough was enough. She stormed into their bedroom, and grabbed Annabel, who was gloating over the newly decorated dresses.

"C'mon," she snapped, and swept her confused sister downstairs, and out to the garden, where Katie was practising dribbling round a line of pot plants.

Becky booted the ball over to the other side of the garden, leaving Katie gaping (she hadn't known Becky could do that!) and headed down the path, still dragging Annabel, and calling over her shoulder, "You can practise later – we need to talk. Come on!"

She shooed both sisters into the guinea-pig

shed. This was for two reasons – it was well away from Mum, so they wouldn't be overheard, and it was Becky's own territory. If she was going to stand any chance of bossy Katie and mouthy Annabel listening to what she had to say, she needed to be somewhere she felt confident. She slammed the door and leaned against it, breathing fast. The other two were giving her an identical funny look – a "what's she playing at?" look. Becky didn't do things like this.

She scowled back. "I've got something to say, and you two are going to listen to me without arguing, or interrupting, or telling me to shut up and stop being stupid, which is what you've been doing for the last fortnight. You just keep on ignoring me!"

Katie and Annabel gaped back at her. What had got into her suddenly? She sounded more like Katie than Katie did sometimes.

"Do you know where Mum is?" Becky had her arms folded, and she was doing a scary impression of Mr Hatton, their monster French teacher.

"Um, no. . ." Katie ventured.

"Bel?"

"Er, upstairs?"

"Uh-huh. She's upstairs, in her room, crying – because of us! Because *we* made her split up with Max's dad!"

"No, we didn't!" argued Annabel automatically.

"OK – so why do you think she did it then?"

Annabel shrugged. "Irreconcilable differences, I suppose." It was what one of her favourite actresses had said last week about her marriage breaking up.

"Yeah – and you're one of them. They split up because we couldn't get on with Max. Lunch today made them see it was never going to work."

Annabel shuffled her feet, guiltily. But Katie wasn't so easy. "So what were we supposed to do? Pretend it's fine that she's dating Max's dad, and he's our best mate? I'm not going to *lie*, Becky." She assumed a virtuous, smug, totally annoying expression.

Becky took a deep breath, to stop herself wanting to throw a guinea-pig hutch at her sister's head. "I'm saying, why don't you stop being so selfish and start thinking about other people for once!"

Katie rolled her eyes. "Here we go!"

"You're only making out that I'm being stupid because you're too scared to listen," said Becky flatly.

Katie's eyes snapped back to her. "Go on then!"

"Right. Well, for a start, you've made Mum really miserable, and in case you hadn't noticed, she was looking happier than she had for ages – maybe she needed somebody, you know! It's not up to you who she goes out with. And second, I know you hate Max, and I don't like him either, but this is worse for him than it is for us."

"Oh, come on, how do you make that out?" scoffed Annabel.

"You know his Mum died?"

"Well, yeah. . ." Annabel muttered – it wasn't fair of Becky to bring that up. You had to give someone automatic sympathy when something as awful as that had happened to them, which was difficult when you hated their guts.

"This is the first time his dad has dated anyone since then, and he feels like his dad's forgotten all about his mum. OK, so we miss our dad and we don't get to see him that often, but nothing so awful has happened to us. Has it?" She rounded on Katie, who was still scowling. "And I don't care what you say, you've been just as bad as he has lately!"

Katie shrugged, but she looked embarrassed, and maybe ever so slightly ashamed of herself. "So what do you want us to do then?" she muttered.

"I don't want you to do anything," Becky replied irritably. "There's no way you can pretend to suddenly like Max now. You're just going to have to stay out of his way. I'm going to talk to him at school tomorrow, and we're going to get Mum and his dad back together."

Katie scowled, but didn't disagree – Becky's harsh words had had their effect.

Becky looked at Annabel, who was also frowning.

"You've really thought about this, haven't you?" Annabel asked. "I mean, I've just been trying to forget about it and hoping it would go away – but it just isn't. I suppose you're right. I hate that you are, but I think we're going to have to go along with it. Is talking to Max about all this a good idea though?" she added doubtfully. "I mean, look what happened when you tried to talk to him last time – a massive bust-up."

Becky folded her arms, and looked determined – in fact, she looked exactly like Katie. "The mood I'm in right now, I don't care what he does. He's *going* to listen. Anyway, what were the chances of me talking you two round?"

Katie and Annabel looked sheepish.

"So if I can get you two to do what I want, I reckon I can sort out one Max. Although it might be quite nice if you weren't far away, just in case he tries to tear me into little pieces. . ."

Becky had been expecting to have to fight her corner all over again the next morning, when Katie and Annabel had had a bit more time to think up some good arguments. Surprisingly, though, they didn't say anything, and Becky noticed Annabel watching Mum worriedly as she stirred her coffee over and over again at breakfast.

Katie brought the subject up on the way to school. "So, when are you going to talk to Max then?" Her voice didn't sound as though she exactly approved of the plan, but she wasn't saying it was over her dead body.

"Not sure. What do you think?" Becky asked, hoping to get Katie involved in the planning – surely that would make her less angry about it?

Katie just shrugged, and wandered moodily on. Becky directed a despairing glance at Annabel, who rolled her eyes. "I reckon you'd better talk to him in the playground. Try and find him before school. That way you won't have people crowding all round you, like you would in the classroom – you don't want Amy and her lot eavesdropping, do you?"

Becky shook her head – no, this was going to be embarrassing enough already. "You will come and hover, won't you? I don't want you to talk to him for me, or anything, just wait round the corner or something."

"Course," said Annabel putting an arm round Becky's shoulders. "Won't we, Katie?"

Katie's grumpy march ahead was carefully calculated so she could still hear everything that was going on. "S'pose," she muttered.

But her reluctance seemed to melt away when the triplets reached the school gates, and spotted Max sitting on the steps to the dining hall, gazing into space. She moved in close to Becky, and said, "Just don't let him get away with anything. We'll be watching, remember? If he starts being a prat we'll come and get him."

Becky smiled at her, and nodded. There was no point saying that "getting" Max was part of the whole problem – Katie was making a big effort as it was.

She walked over to Max, fiddling nervously with the strap on her rucksack, and stood in front of him until he looked up aggressively. He seemed to be angry with everyone these days. "You again!" he snarled. "Get away from me, you stupid dumb blonde."

Becky ignored this, and the temptation to say that stupid and dumb were the same thing. She stared back at him, trying to think herself strong. *Remember making Katie and Bel listen to you! Remember Mum's face this morning!*

Max had obviously been hoping she'd just

scuttle off as soon as he opened his mouth. His face darkened, and he stood up, still on the steps so he towered over her. "Get – out – of – my – face!"

"No," Becky said calmly. "I need you to listen, then I'll go."

"You listen! I'm not talking to you, any of you. Me and my dad don't want anything to do with you!"

"That isn't true."

"What?" Max sounded confused.

"We don't like you, and you *hate* us, but your dad and our mum really like each other. They only said they'd stop seeing each other because we were fighting so much." She paused. "I'm sorry. I know it's really awful for you – with your mum and everything. . ." She trailed off as Max's eyes blazed.

"What do you know about my mum?"

Becky faltered. It was so difficult to talk about this – what was she supposed to say to him?

"Well, that she – that she—"

"Died. You can't even say it, can you?" Max sneered.

"I'm sorry," Becky whispered, feeling terrible. She tried to summon back some of the strength she'd had moments before. She was sure that she was doing the right thing – she just had to get the words out. "Look, I heard what you were saying to Lucky yesterday."

Max went rigid. "What? When?"

Becky shuffled in embarrassment – after all, she had been spying. "When you were on the stairs, holding him."

What little colour had been in Max's face drained away entirely. He looked as though he wanted to kill her. It ran through Becky's mind, very quickly, as she tried to stand her ground, that he *had* been crying, and he knew she'd seen him, and that was what he couldn't stand.

Max was balling his hands into fists. His face was so angry that Becky actually wondered whether he was going to hit her, or grab her by the shoulders and shove her over, just to get her out of his way. Then suddenly he seemed to sag, and he slumped down on the steps as though he didn't care any more.

Becky looked worriedly at him. He seemed so wretched, but he wasn't going to want sympathy from her — was he? She decided she had to go with her instincts. She sat down beside him on the steps. Katie and Annabel, who had been watching from round the corner of one of the classrooms, where they were mostly out of sight, gaped at each other. Until now they hadn't really been able to see what was going on, although they'd nearly dashed over to help out when Max jumped up looking so angry.

Becky continued to speak to Max in a low, soothing voice. "I'm really sorry. I shouldn't have been listening, but I heard Lucky whining, and he's so cute, I wanted to say hello to him. And then I heard you — it was an accident."

Max sniffed.

"It's true, you know, about our parents. They do like each other. They still will, even if we make it so they can't go out – they'll just be really miserable as well."

Max muttered something, and Becky bent closer to hear. "Don't want him to go out with *anyone*."

"Mmm, I know, nor do we. Our mum, I mean."

Max said nothing, but the atmosphere between them wasn't uncomfortable. They sat silently thinking for a moment, and then he said, "Dad didn't even notice when I fed Lucky toast this morning. Normally he goes ballistic if he sees me doing that."

Becky nodded wisely, thinking of Mum stirring her coffee at the breakfast table as though the triplets weren't even there.

"What are we going to do?" Max seemed to have given up.

"You have to get your dad to come to the

wedding." Becky knew that Katie and Annabel weren't going to be too happy about this, but it was the perfect opportunity. "Don't worry, you don't have to come. Just your dad – I'll talk to my aunt about it, it'll be fine. We don't tell my mum, she just sees him there and she's all surprised."

Max sniffed again, as though he didn't think much of the plan, but Becky felt it was more for show than anything else. "Just because we're doing this, it doesn't mean I actually like you, you know. I'm just doing this to make my dad happy."

Becky nodded – she wasn't looking for a friend either. "Will you talk to your dad?"

He shrugged. "Mmm."

"Good. So tell us tomorrow what he said. I'll phone Auntie Jan." And Becky got up decisively and headed back to her sisters, feeling incredibly proud of herself. She noticed that David had arrived and was standing with them, and speeded up slightly.

She'd just had a good idea of how he could help out too — it might take a little persuasion though. . .

As Becky had expected, Katie and Annabel weren't pleased about Mr Cooper coming to the wedding — but at least it was only him and not Max. They were still so surprised by Becky coming over all bossy that they only complained half-heartedly.

They phoned Auntie Jan that evening, and when she realized who it was, she seemed a little strange, as though she was annoyed. Becky guessed that Mum had been crying on her shoulder.

"Is it important, Becky? I'm still at work."

Becky took a deep breath. "Yes, it is. Very. You have to re-invite somebody to the wedding."

"What?"

"Mum's friend — Jeff Cooper. She's probably got you to take him off the list, hasn't she? Well, you have to put him back on."

Auntie Jan's voice was noticeably warmer as she said, "But she told me they'd split up."

"I know, and it was all our fault. Did she tell you about it? About the thing with Max?"

"Yes. She was really upset, Becky."

"I know! But we're going to sort it out. I talked to Max, and he's going to ask his dad to come. We'll make it a surprise for her. Please, Auntie Jan!"

"I hope you know what you're doing."

"We do, we really do, honestly. We're going to sort it all out."

"OK, then. But he'd better turn up, Becky. I'm not having my seating plan mucked up!" Auntie Jan was laughing as she said this – she was obviously really pleased about their idea. Becky did have a slightly worrying thought as she hung up though. Auntie Jan *had* been joking about the seating plan, but she was being a bit of a control freak about her wedding – just what was she going to think of the new-look bridesmaids' dresses?

Chapter Ten

Max's dad agreed to the plan practically before Max had got the words out, he reported grumpily the next day. His dad was delighted that the triplets had decided to try and sort things out, and really keen to get back together with their mum. Max was talking only to Becky, and doing his best to pretend that Annabel, and even more so Katie, just didn't exist.

"Good. So what are you going to do on Saturday? Are you going to stay with someone?"

Max's scowl deepened. "My grandma. I'll be looking at my cousins' baby photos all day. Dad had better be grateful."

Becky turned to David, who was standing behind her looking shifty, and gave him a meaningful stare. He rolled his eyes at her, but the stare only intensified.

"Oh, all right," he muttered. "Max, my mum says you can come over to ours on Saturday afternoon if you want. She said maybe we could go to LaserQuest. Don't feel you have to, or anything. . ." He trailed off, trying not to sound too inviting. He didn't really get on with Max, and he was only doing this because Becky had begged him, and then threatened, and then begged again.

Apparently, even LaserQuesting with someone who was clearly not that eager to have you was better than endless photos of baby cousins. Max agreed as keenly as his dad had.

Becky grinned at them both happily. Finally it felt like she'd done everything she could to make the wedding a success, *and* make things up to Mum – now, hopefully, all they had to do was enjoy the day.

*

It felt weird and exciting waking up on Saturday morning in a hotel room. Becky scrambled out of bed and dashed to the window. Yes! Perfect blue sky, just a few little puffball clouds. She looked out over the hotel gardens, which were so tidy she would have sworn the gardeners cut the grass with nail scissors. The wedding photos were going to be beautiful here. There was even a peacock stalking across the lawn as though he owned the place.

Annabel joined her at the window, yawning. "It's not raining, is it?" she asked worriedly.

"No, look – Auntie Jan's so lucky. We haven't had a day this nice the whole year so far."

"I said it would be," pronounced Annabel smugly. "I suppose we shouldn't start getting ready quite yet, what do you think?"

"Bel! The wedding's not till three! At least can't we have breakfast?" Becky protested.

"Mmm. S'pose."

Breakfast turned out to be a bit of a trial. Katie had hardly moaned all week about the dressing up she was going to have to do (well, only a couple of times a day, anyway), but now she was sitting across the table from their gran, Mum and Auntie Jan's mum, who was not being particularly tactful. Even their grandad was trying to signal with his eyebrows as Gran prattled on.

"Oh, it'll be so lovely, seeing you three in little matching frocks. There's nothing prettier than my little granddaughters when you're dressed right. Proper dresses, not jeans and those horrible football shirts. I haven't seen you in a dress for years, Katie dear."

Katie, wearing jeans and a football shirt, was looking less and less like someone who would be happily walking down an aisle in a pretty dress a few hours from now. She laid her half-eaten piece of toast on her plate and glared at Gran.

Grandad diplomatically intervened by

prompting Gran to tell Auntie Jan which hat she'd decided to buy in the end. The answer, together with full descriptions of all the hats Gran *hadn't* bought, took the rest of the meal.

Despite the wedding not being until three, Mum and Auntie Jan really did seem to think that getting ready should start right after breakfast. Katie was looking distinctly woebegone — although Annabel, listening to the timetable of hairdressing, manicures and full makeovers, seemed positively blissed out.

"We don't need to get our hair done right now, do we?" wheedled Becky. "The hairdresser could do Annabel first?"

"I suppose so. . ." said Mum, looking thoughtfully at Katie. Maybe it *was* asking for trouble to make her sit in the room with perfect hair for any longer than necessary.

"Right." Becky dashed over to her bag, grabbed something, and then seized Katie's hand. "We'll be back in an hour, OK?"

"Where are we going?" wailed Katie, as

Becky raced her down the corridor to the lift.

"Did you read the hotel brochure?"

"No!" Katie sounded somewhat disgusted. She'd been avoiding the wedding as much as possible, Becky knew that.

"Well, it's got a swimming pool, and a whirlpool thing – I thought you'd like that more than watching other people having their hair done. Come on, I brought our cozzies, but we haven't got long!"

The swimming had been a brainwave. The two of them splashed and chased each other till they were completely out of breath, and then floated in the whirlpool till they felt well and truly relaxed. They even peeped into the sauna, but they couldn't see the attraction in burning your bottom on a hot bench in a room where you could hardly breathe.

When they got back, Annabel was sitting regally in a chair, wearing a somewhat–large white towelling robe, gazing happily into a mirror while her hair was coaxed into a complicated updo complete with trailing curls. She grinned at Katie. "It's OK. You don't have to have your hair like this if you don't want. I persuaded Auntie Jan it would be nice if our hair wasn't *exactly* the same. I think Gran going on and on at breakfast made her think that us all being totally identical would be a bit scary."

Katie breathed a deep sigh of relief. She wasn't sure Annabel was even going to be able to *see* with her hair like that. She was feeling so deliciously floppy after the swim, though, that the whole beauty routine was almost bearable. She could shut her eyes and float away for a lot of it, anyway.

Becky smiled to herself. Mission accomplished – one de-stressed Katie, as ready as she'd ever be to be zipped into a gorgeous dress.

An hour and a half later, after a hurried sandwich lunch from room service, and then the finishing touches of make-up, the dress-bags were taken out of the wardrobe. Auntie

Jan was in her own room getting ready, so it was just Mum, who was already in her wedding outfit, helping the triplets.

They held their breath as she brought out the first dress — Annabel's, the original rat-customized disaster. What would she say?

Mum unzipped the bodice and held the dress for Annabel to step into — there was no way she was risking that hairdo by slipping it over her head. Then she zipped it up, and stood back to admire.

"You look beautiful, Bel. This dress is so pretty." She held her head on one side. "There looks to be something different about it today, but I can't think what. It must be that lovely hairdo. OK, come on, Becky."

The triplets exchanged amazed, relieved glances. If Mum hadn't even noticed, they couldn't have messed the dresses up that badly!

Once she'd got all three of them into the dresses, Mum popped next door to see how

Auntie Jan was getting on, leaving the triplets with strict instructions not even to move unless they had to.

"I can't believe she didn't notice!" Annabel sounded almost disappointed.

Katie smiled grimly. "Don't worry. Auntie Jan will."

Becky wasn't listening. She touched Katie's elbow gently. "Look!" she breathed. The wardrobe had a big mirror on the door, and Becky had just caught sight of their reflection.

"Wow!" Katie murmured, all thoughts of horrified aunts disappearing from her mind. *"Wow!"*

It was pretty amazing. Although their hair was different, and they'd followed Fran's idea and worked slightly different colours into the beading on each dress, the triplets' outfits were almost identical – and they looked wonderful. Far better than they had at the fittings, now that they had the hair and make-up, shoes and bags – and Katie wasn't scowling.

The three of them stared, awestruck, and that was how Auntie Jan found them when she and the photographer came to fetch them for the first photos. They were so entranced, even Katie, that they jumped when she appeared in the mirror behind them. They'd forgotten all about the altered dresses, and they beamed round at her delightedly as she put her arms round the three of them.

"You match us very nicely," said Annabel, sounding as purry as a cat.

"Bel! Other way round!" scolded Becky. "The dress is beautiful, Auntie Jan."

"So are yours. But — where did the beads come from? I'm sure they were plain when we picked them up from the dressmaker, weren't they, Sue?" She turned to the triplets' mum, looking confused.

"Oh! So that's what it is. I couldn't work it out."

Mum and Auntie Jan looked at the triplets questioningly, and Annabel poked Becky. It was definitely up to her to explain!

"I'm sorry, Auntie Jan, I know you wanted the dresses plain, but we had a – a sort of *accident*. . ."

"Huh," muttered Annabel.

"My rats escaped and they ate Annabel's dress," Becky blurted out – it was easier than pussyfooting around.

"The beads are to disguise the holes," Annabel added helpfully, as Auntie Jan had gone white under her make-up. "Look." She twirled. "You can't see them at all. And I think the dresses are prettier, this way. I do, honestly."

"You girls did this?" Auntie Jan sounded as though she couldn't believe it.

"Uh-huh. Saima and the others helped though. It's nice, isn't it? We worked out the design ourselves and everything."

"I'm amazed." Auntie Jan shook her head. "I'm almost grateful to your rats, Becky – the dresses were beautiful before, but now they're really special. You should be so proud of yourselves."

The photographer coughed meaningfully from the doorway, and Auntie Jan grinned. "Come on, you three – smile!"

A little while later (the photographer was really good, and the photos actually *hadn't* taken that long) the triplets and Auntie Jan and Grandad were gathered in the church porch, giggling with nerves. It was so funny – all those people in there waiting for them! Then the music started, Auntie Jan shook out the skirt of her dress one last time, Grandad grinned at the triplets, and they were off, walking slowly down the aisle.

Annabel was in her element, with everyone staring, but even Becky and Katie rather enjoyed it. Somehow the hair and make-up, and above all the wonderful dresses, made them feel like different people, people who didn't mind being the centre of attention. *I wouldn't like it all the time*, Becky thought. *But it's very nice just once in a while!*

Suddenly Annabel nudged her gently. "Look!" she whispered, out of the corner of her mouth.

Becky looked where Annabel was looking. It was Mum – and Jeff was standing next to her, both of them beaming. The plan had worked! As they came up to the front, Becky exchanged satisfied smiles with the other two, and then kept a small, very contented smile of her own. There had been disasters along the way, but here they all were at last. Auntie Jan was going to have the best wedding ever!

Have you read all the
Triplets books?
Turn the page for a sneak peek
of the first book in the series!

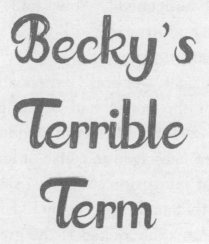

Becky's
Terrible
Term

It was half-past seven on the first morning of the new school year – and things were not going to plan in the Ryan house.

"Mum! Where's my pencil case?"

"And my PE kit?"

"And my other shoe?"

Three excited and slightly panicky voices spoke at once, and Mrs Ryan looked round from the kitchen counter in horror. "What on earth's happened? You had everything yesterday – it can't all have disappeared overnight."

Sometimes, generally when all the floor-space in the house had disappeared under piles of washing, Mrs Ryan wondered how her daughters managed to cause at least ten girls' worth of confusion. What was it about the triplets that made them seem like three blonde hurricanes? She looked at the girls scurrying round the kitchen in a panic and laughed. At least she got more than three times the fun as well!

"Your shoe's there, Becky, under the table, look."

"I definitely didn't leave it there — I wish you'd play football with your *own* shoes, Katie. It's always mine that end up kicked into stupid places."

"I'm *wearing* my shoes, silly. You shouldn't leave them lying around — it's too tempting. Where is that pencil case, I know I had it. . ."

Katie rummaged around on the kitchen table, rootling through Mrs Ryan's newspaper, and threatening to disturb the large pile of her mother's filing that was towering in the middle of the big pine table.

"Oh, Katie, I was reading that! And please don't knock that pile over, I'd just sorted it — oh, well," Mrs Ryan sighed. "Look — your pencil case is here, in your bag where you put it last night. Honestly, you three, I think you all need glasses. Annabel, what did you say you'd lost?"

"My PE kit, but I haven't, Orlando's sitting on it. Get off, you great lump!"

Annabel tugged at her purple PE bag, trying to dislodge the fat ginger cat who'd decided that her tracksuit and trainers were definitely comfier than his expensive cat basket. Orlando yawned, and stretched, and then shook out his fearsomely clawed paws as slowly as he could. He gave Annabel a look of total contempt and strolled over to Becky to see if he could get a second breakfast out of her.

"Come here, Orlando," said Becky, picking him up and rubbing her face against his ears, starting a rumbling purr from somewhere deep inside him. "Ignore that awful Annabel, she doesn't love you at all, does she?"

"Huh. When that cat apologizes for being sick on my best T-shirt, then I might just decide to like him again. But I'm still waiting. Fleabag!" Annabel hissed, mock-furiously.

Orlando hissed back, and then turned his "I'm starving" face on Becky, and gave a piteous little mew.

"Uh-uh," said Becky. "I'm not falling for it

today, puss. I know I've fed you. It's your own fault if you ate the whole bowl in ten seconds flat." She tapped his nose with one finger firmly. "No more food!"

Orlando wriggled crossly till Becky put him down, and then stalked off to sulk in next door's garden. Maybe today would be the day that all his hours of watching their bird table finally paid off.

"Sit down and eat your breakfast, you three. You need to have plenty to keep you going. I should think you'll be running about all over the place," said Mum, sipping her coffee.

"I'm really glad that we went to the Open Evening," said Katie. "At least we know where we're going. I think I do, anyway."

"Well, I can't remember anything," said Annabel. "Except that all the corridors had paint the colour of sick."

"Uurrgh! Bel, that's disgusting. I was going to have some muesli and now you've really put me off." Becky pushed her bowl away, shuddering. Her stomach wasn't happy anyway, as all her nervousness about the new school seemed to be having a party in there, but now she felt even worse.

"I don't know how you can eat that stuff, anyway. It looks *exactly* like the mix you give the guinea pigs. It's probably just the same thing in a different packet."

"Except I think the guinea-pig food costs more," put in Mum. "Your zoo in the shed is eating us out of house and home, Becky."

Becky grinned. She knew Mum didn't mean it. She loved having all the animals around. It wasn't just Orlando and the guinea pigs – there was Pixie, the little black cat who'd turned up in the garden one morning two years ago, and stayed, and every so often a bird that Becky had rescued, generally from Pixie, who was a ruthless hunter. Becky thought it might be because Pixie had lived as a stray – she wasn't used to two delicious bowls of Whiskas a day, and she liked her food on the move.

"How about some toast instead?" Mum offered.

"OK. I'll put some on – anyone else?" said Becky, jumping up. Perhaps a piece of toast would help her feel less weird.

Annabel looked longingly at the loaf that Becky was waving at her in a tempting fashion. "Nope," she said finally. "Can't manage it."

"I'm not surprised. You practically inhaled that cereal," said Katie. "I'll have some, please, Becky. Can you pass the peanut butter, too?"

Mrs Ryan started to assemble three packed lunches from the fridge. "So you think you know where your classroom is, Katie?" she said.

"Yes, I think so. And the hall. And I definitely know how to get to the playing fields. They looked excellent. Loads more space than our old school. I can't wait."

Annabel looked at her sister sadly. "Mad.

Probably got hit on the head by a football – a tragic case."

"Huh. Well, at least I've got some clue where I'm going. Can you remember anything? Oh no, course not – there's no clothes shops at school. And Becky'll only know where there's a bird's nest in the playground. It'll be me looking after the two of you, *as usual*."

Katie was quite right. She was much the most organized of the triplets, and she did tend to lead the other two around. The triplets might look identical, but their characters were totally different. Katie, confident and a bit bossy, Annabel, a head-in-the-clouds, happy-go-lucky show-off, and Becky, the shyest and most thoughtful of the three.

And of course, thought Mrs Ryan, as she surveyed the fridge, *they* would *all like different food*. Had she got it all in the right boxes? One purple and silver lunchbox with cheese sandwiches, one Manchester United lunchbox with ham, and one blue box with a kitten on, with cheese *and* ham. At least they all liked granary bread – this week, anyway!

Mrs Ryan finished her coffee, then noticed the time and panicked. "You'd better have one last check that you've got everything, girls, and then put your jumpers on. It's nearly quarter-past eight."

Becky and Katie licked toast crumbs off their fingers and went to put their plates in the sink.

"Are you working at home today, Mum?" asked Annabel, running her spoon round her cereal bowl for the last few drops of milk. Mrs Ryan worked as a translator, translating books in French and German into English, and the other way round. Most days she worked at home, but about once a week she went into an office. It was a good system, as it meant she was able to fit in work and looking after the triplets.

"Yes, I'll be here all day. I'm in the office for

a meeting on Thursday. I've got a lot to do this week."

"Excellent. Does that mean we get to cook dinner?" asked Annabel. She loved to cook – especially cakes that she could decorate afterwards – and then eat! The others loved to cook, too, but it generally ended up with Becky doing the washing up, after Katie had fought with Annabel to try and make her clean up her own mess.

"Mmm, I could certainly do with some help. Of course, I'll have to fit in the shopping first. Any requests?"

"Fish fingers. Can we have them for tonight's tea?" asked Katie.

"We're nearly out of crisps, too. And can we have some more of those minty biscuits?" added Annabel.

"You're such a junk-food freak," said Becky. "Don't forget the cat food this time, Mum."

"Hang on, hang on, I need to write this

down. Biscuits, yes," muttered Mrs Ryan, grabbing a pad from by the kitchen phone. "Cat food. . ."

"Come *on*, Mum, if you're sure you really want to come." Katie had her arms folded, and was looking impatient.

"Of course I'm coming with you on your first morning! Get your things together, girls, we'd better be off. Manor Hill is a bit further away than your old school."

"I'm glad we can still walk though," said Katie, closing the front gate behind her, and patting Pixie, who'd managed to squash herself on to the gatepost. "Watch it, Pixie – move one paw a centimetre and you'll be in a real state. I don't know how she can sit there like that – it can't be comfy."

"I think she's just proving she can!" giggled Becky, as they all headed up the road towards their new school.

Look out for more

HOLLY WEBB

Triplets

Becky's Terrible Term

HOLLY WEBB

Triplets

Annabel's Perfect Party

HOLLY WEBB

Triplets

Katie's Big Match

HOLLY WEBB

Triplets

Becky's Problem Pet

HOLLY WEBB

Triplets

Annabel's Starring Role

HOLLY WEBB

Triplets

Katie's Secret Admirer

Look out for

Animal Magic

Look out for

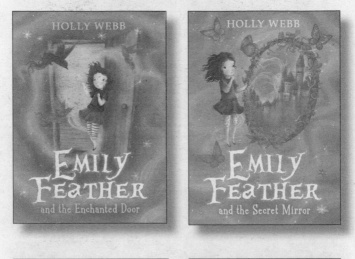

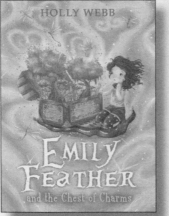

HOLLY has always loved animals.
As a child, she had two dogs, a cat, and at
one point, nine gerbils (an accident).
Holly's other love is books. Holly now lives
in Reading with her husband, three sons
and a very spoilt cat.

TEN QUICK QUESTIONS FOR HOLLY WEBB

1. Kittens or puppies? Kittens

2. Chocolate or Sweets? Chocolate

3. Salad or chips? Chips

4. Favourite websites? Youtube, Lolcats

5. Text or call? Call

6. Favourite lesson at school? Ancient Greek (you did ask. . .)

7. Worst lesson at school? Physics

8. Favourite colour? Green

9. Favourite film? The Sound of Music

10. City or countryside? Countryside, but with fast trains to the city!